REMO H

The Apowa tribesmen were ready to blow up the monument with a .155 millimeter cannon unless Remo delivered the rebels from the Revolutionary Indian Party. But the problem was that the monument masked the Cassandra— an atomic doomsday machine. If Remo failed to stop the attack it could wipe out America by setting off the Cassandra.

And then Remo found that he had another problem. Walking along the dirt road leading from the motel toward the press compound, he met Van Riker, the designer of Cassandra. The general saw Remo and smiled.

"Where's the Oriental?" he asked.

"He's back in his room being propositioned by a Russian agent," said Remo airily.

Van Riker looked surprised, not sure whether or not to believe Remo. Finally he said, "Oh? Who?"

"Valash-something," said Remo.

Van Riker's face turned pale under his tan. "Tell me. Did he say Valashnikov?"

"Yeah, that's it."

"Oh, my God," said Van Riker.

"What's the problem?" Remo asked.

"He was a Russian intelligence officer," Van Riker answered. "His job was to find the Cassandra. This time, he's found it . . ."

The Destroyer Series

THE DESTROYER
LAST WAR DANCE
by Richard Sapir & Warren Murphy

PINNACLE BOOKS • NEW YORK CITY

THE DESTROYER: LAST WAR DANCE

Copyright © 1974 by Richard Sapir and Warren Murphy

All rights reserved, including the right to reproduce this book or portions thereof in any form.

An original Pinnacle Books edition, published for the first time anywhere.

ISBN: 0-523-00435-4

First printing, October 1974

Printed in the United States of America

PINNACLE BOOKS, INC.
275 Madison Avenue
New York, N.Y. 10016

For Geri Flynn, who remembers Chiun in the gray sweater, and for the glorious House of Sinanju, P. O. Box 1149, Pittsfield, Massachusetts.

CHAPTER ONE

Twenty-five feet down they began hitting the bodies. The big scoop that had followed the workers down into the Montana earth, devouring the loosenings of dynamite and pick, spilled out bones from its soil-dripping jaws.

Cracked skulls there were, large and small and some so tiny they looked as if they had come from the necks of monkeys. Limb bones, some cracked, some whole, some smashed into sharp white fragments. You could walk in the crunch of bones that dry summer afternoon in 1961.

The workmen asked if they should stop.

"No," said the government supervisor from Washington. "I don't think so. I'll check, though. Jeez. All in one bunch, huh?"

"So far," said the foreman. "In the last scoop."

"Jeez," said the supervisor again and disappeared into his gray trailer, where everyone knew he had a telephone without a dial that he didn't talk about and a safe hidden under his bunk that he didn't talk about and an assistant who carried a .45 automatic and didn't talk to anyone.

The foreman turned to the workers, who had been standing around waiting for a decision. "Whaddya want from me, already?" he asked in accent that was strange for the prairie country. "You know what kind of a contract dis is. Who else digs hundred-foot holes in da middle of prairies? Don't waste your time waiting for the supervisor. Don't even wait for him. He's going to say, 'Go back to work.' Guaranteed. When he come out of dat trailer, he's going to say, 'Go the other seventy-five feet.' "

A crane-operator climbed down from the cab of his crane and picked up what looked like a fragment of a whitish bowl.

"Who could do such a thing? Who'd wanna do such a thing?" he asked, looking at the remnant of the small head, which fit into the palm of one hand, and at the cracked hole in the back of it. Then he started to cry. He placed it gently on a small rise and refused to dig farther.

"You gotta," said the foreman. "It's part of da contract. No stoppages are allowed on dese kind of contracts. They'll pull your union card."

"You can take your contract and wipe your nose wit' it! Dat crane don't go no farther," he wailed in heavy Brooklynese.

Other machines stopped, and picks stopped, and there was silence in the prairie.

The government supervisor came running out of the gray trailer. "It's all right. It's all right. It's all right," he shouted. "Go ahead. Don't worry about the bones. They're hundreds of years old."

"You hear dat?" yelled the foreman into the hole.

"He says the bones are hundreds and hundreds of years old."

"Then how come dere's a piece of lead in dis skull and a small hole in it? How come, huh?" yelled back one of the workmen. "And here's a woman's beads or something. How come da bullet?"

"Maybe she fell on a piece of lead. How should I know?"

"It ain't hundreds of years."

"So if it's yesterday, already, what do you care?" yelled the foreman.

"Because I care," said the worker.

"You'll never work on one of these again," the government supervisor said angrily. "But all right. If you men have to be shown, we'll find someone who will explain to you that we're not just ignoring a mass murder."

Late that afternoon a U.S. Air Force helicopter settled down on the site, and a white-haired man with a magnificent tan got out. He spoke with the soft quiet of authority and the simplicity of real expertise. There had not been one mass murder there, he said, but two. They had happened thousands of years apart.

The later one occurred in 1873—one of the last Indian battles, if it could be called a battle. A U. S. Cavalry troop searching for a Sioux raiding party came across the peaceful Indian village of Wounded Elk and massacred the men, women, and children. Hence the bullets in some of the skulls.

This happened at the time when the government was first becoming ashamed of its treatment of the

Indians. So the massacre was kept quiet, and the punishment for the cavalry troop was to dig a hole fifty feet deep and bury the incriminating evidence.

But at twenty-five feet they discovered older bones, and the captain ordered them to dig no farther but to bury the victims at that level.

"Where'd da older bones come from?" demanded the crane-operator.

"Well, do you see that child's skull over there on that little mound?" asked the white-haired man, pointing to the head that had brought the recent tears. "It was killed in Indian fashion. They would grab a child by its feet and bash its head against a rock."

The crane-operator looked disgusted. "Dat's awful," he said. "When'd dat happen?"

"The best estimate is between ten and fifteen thousand years ago. Those are rough parameters, but in this prairie, twenty-five feet down equals roughly fifteen thousand years. Indians didn't bury their massacres beneath the ground you see. They left them on ground level." His voice carried that little dancing joy of amusement, but there was no other amusement at the deep prairie hole.

Eyebrows were furrowed, and the eyes of these men with rough, weathered faces showed deep pity. Fifteen thousand, a hundred thousand years meant little when they thought about someone swinging a baby by its feet to bash its head against a rock.

"In da later massacree," began a man, leaning thick arms on the handle of a pick, "the one with da calvary . . . how come youse guys know about it, when

4

da government wanted to keep it like, secret, you know. How come?"

"Yeah, how come?" asked the crane-operator.

The white-haired man smiled as if a clear fact were always a pleasure, even when it concerned the murder of a baby. "It is in the archives of the old Department of the Army, which is now the Department of Defense. We knew where this site was, but we didn't think you'd hit it exactly. The odds against hitting it exactly were millions to one, considering the original location was fixed by star and by very distant landmark. This is a big, big prairie."

"Yeah. You can say dat again. I ain't sure where da hell we are," said the crane-operator.

"You're not supposed to," said the foreman. "Whaddya think, dey got us city guys on dis job because dey like Brooklyn or something? A shit-kicker might know just where he is. C'mon. Let's go. You got your answer. Back to woik."

The crane-operator returned to his cab, and other machines started. The helicopter left the prairie, where there was again the hammering noise of civilization.

The workmen continued for two weeks, digging to exact specifications, and then went on to another site, hundreds of miles away, where they dug another hole, whose only purpose was to confuse them about the location of the first.

The supervisor from Washington and his quiet assistant with the gun stayed on at the first hole. After the excavators came the men who built the metal structure for the concrete. And after the concrete was

5

poured, a perfectly round hole hardened exactly one hundred eleven feet deep in the Montana prairie. The supervisor and the man with the gun stayed on.

After the concrete came the skilled technicians who completed the wiring for the giant underground silo. And after them, in three stages, on Air Force flatbed trucks, came the missile. Putting it in place was like constructing an eleven-story building underground with a jeweler's loupe. This too was completed, and the supervisor and the man with the gun watched the technicians go.

It was winter when the large box came in the tractor-trailer. The driver was the white-haired man who had answered the diggers' questions. His tan was still magnificent.

When he entered the gray trailer, the government supervisor stood to attention. "General Van Riker, sir," said the supervisor.

The white-haired man blew the chill from his fingertips. He nodded toward the safe, whose dial peeked out from under a bunk.

"Do you understand all that?" he asked.

"I've had time to study it, sir," said the supervisor.

General Van Riker looked to the quiet man who carried the gun. The man nodded.

"All right," said Van Riker, lowering himself lightly into a folding steel chair. "You know, we almost canceled during that bone incident. You should have prepared for the possibility of the bodies. I shouldn't have had to come here before I was supposed to."

The government supervisor raised his hands in a shrug. "For all the workmen know, this is an ordinary

6

missile with an ordinary head. They were spooked by the bones, that's all. The crane-operator held a little funeral for one skull, I think, the day after you left."

"I know they think it's an ordinary ICBM. That's not the problem. I just don't want this to be the silo they remember. That's why I've sent them all over these prairies, digging more holes. Just to confuse them. But that's neither your worry nor your fault."

General Van Riker nodded to the safe again. "C'mon, we'll need that."

From the safe the supervisor brought two clipboards with notes and diagrams. General Van Riker recognized them immediately. He had written them. He had never commanded so much as an infantry platoon or a single airplane, but he had written those plans. And on the day he devised a two-man, two-day all-weather installation of an underground missile—as opposed to the usual method requiring multitudes and weeks and ideal conditions—he had been promoted to lieutenant general in the United States Air Force from a laboratory in an Atomic Energy Commission installation.

Before he had left his civilian post in the AEC lab, Van Riker had also designed something else—what one think-tank scientist called "the loser warhead" because "you use it when you lose one of two things: a world war or your sanity."

Now in this Montana prairie Van Riker was bringing both his theories together.

The supervisor donned his cold-weather gear, and with the clipboards under one arm, he joined General

7

Van Riker and stepped out into the subzero winter night.

The quiet man who carried the gun watched the two go to the truck and back it up to the tarpaulin-covered silo. He turned off the light in the little trailer to let his eyes adjust to the darkness but all he saw was a large metal arm extending from the back of the van. A large, dark canopy seemed to glide slowly along what appeared to be a pulley device on the arm, finally stopping over the tarpaulin.

In the morning the quiet man saw that the dark canopy was a small air-filled workshed. Van Riker and the supervisor emerged only to grab a few hours sleep when darkness fell again. Then they went back to the canopy workshed.

On the second day when darkness fell again, General Van Riker returned to the trailer and said to the quiet man, "Go ahead. Do you want a drink first?"

"Not during work," the quiet man said.

"How about after?"

"I drink bourbon. Make it a double." The quiet man unholstered his .45 caliber automatic, checked the clip and the chamber, dry-fired it once, then returned it to its shoulder holster with the safety off.

"I know you drink bourbon," said Van Riker. "You drink a lot of it."

"Not when I'm dry."

"I know that, too. You have long periods of abstinence. You're very capable of it."

"Thank you," said the quiet man.

And Van Riker smiled his joy-of-fact smile, the same smile that came from knowing that the Montana prairie contained the bones of two massacres and that at twenty-five feet in this prairie the original bones must be about fifteen thousand years old.

Outside, the quiet man felt the chilling nip of the Montana winter night, felt the canopy of ice-clear stars above him, and crunched his way forward in moonlight so bright he could almost read in it.

"Oh" was all he said when he saw the site. Where the tarpaulin and then the workshed had been was now a huge block of marble five feet high and stretching almost fifty feet across. A giant block of statuary marble in the middle of a prairie. Rising about a foot and a half above it was something dark. He went to the marble, which came up to his chin, and saw that the something dark appeared to be a round brass cylinder.

"Up here," came the supervisor's voice. "I'm up here. General Van Riker said you're supposed to help."

When the quiet man hoisted himself up onto the block of marble, he saw that he was standing next to a giant bronze circle, which appeared to have raised letters.

It was a giant plaque. It felt funny to walk across the lettering. He had never walked on a plaque before, and he wondered absently whether the raised letters were cutting into the soles of his boots.

He motioned to the supervisor that he wanted the clipboards, then took them silently and clipped them securely to his belt.

"Van Riker said that when I gave you those clipboards, you would explain the reason for those two

9

holes over there," said the supervisor, pointing to the other side of the marble base, where there were two dark holes, three feet in diameter, like mini-silos. "There's no reason in these plans for them, But General Van Riker said they were essential and that you'd tell me."

The quiet man nodded for the supervisor to accompany him across the plaque to the holes.

"Will you say something?" demanded the supervisor angrily. "Van Riker says you're going to give me an explanation. I told him it would be the first time I ever heard you talk. Now, talk."

The quiet man looked at the three-foot holes and then at the supervisor he had lived with for so long without looking, without talking, making an effort not to listen to anything more important than a request to pass the salt. He had even stolen the picture of the supervisor's family that had been on his desk because he did not wish to look at the three young boys and smiling woman. He had thrown the picture, frame and all, into the maximum-disposal bags that were burned at the site every day.

"There's a reason why I didn't talk to you all this time," said the quiet man. "I didn't want to get to know you."

He brought the .45 out of his shoulder holster and put the first bullet between the supervisor's eyes. The heavy slug sent the head snapping back, as if a baseball bat had collided with it. The body followed. The supervisor hit the plaque. The body twitched violently and then was still. The quiet man returned

10

the gun to the holster but did not put on the safety catch.

He dragged the supervisor's feet over to one of the holes on the side of the marble monument, then dropped the feet over the edge. He grabbed the shoulders and pushed them toward the feet, and the supervisor's corpse slid down into the hole, his head only eighteen inches from the top of the bronze plaque, which looked like a giant blowup of a penny atop a match box.

When the quiet man reached for his .45 again, he felt the wetness of the handle and realized his hands were covered with blood. He knelt on the plaque and leaned down into the hole, the gun stretched out in front of him. When it touched the supervisor's head, he fired three times. The splattering bone fragments, brain, and blood gushed up into the quiet man's face as he fired the last rounds of certainty.

"Shit," he said, putting the sticky gun back into the holster.

"Did he fight back?" asked General Van Riker when he saw the bloody face and right arm of the quiet man.

"No. I just got some of him back at me when I put in my certainty shots. It's a mess."

"Here's your drink. Without ice because I figured you had enough cold out there. The clipboards, please."

The quiet man took the glass and looked at it. He did not drink.

"How come there are two holes, General?"

11

"The other is kind of a filter chamber for the first one. Bodies tend to rot and smell, you know."

"Well, I was thinking . . . since you're obviously the guy who designed that missile warhead . . . I mean, I'm no expert on missiles, but I know that two men in two days don't install ordinary warheads. I mean, that had to be some kind of specially designed warhead. As little as I know, I know you don't arm a missile like you put a bullet in the chamber of a gun."

Van Riker interrupted. "So what you're saying is you think that anyone who could design that sort of easily installed warhead could certainly design a single burial cylinder, and you suspect the second cylinder is for you. Correct?"

"Well, yeah. Correct."

"And you think we killed the supervisor like the pharaohs used to kill the workers who constructed the pyramids."

"Well, sort of."

"Do you know what kind of warhead that is?" asked Van Riker.

"No."

"Do you know whether it's even nuclear?"

"No."

"See? You don't know enough to be killed. All you know is that it's something special and where it is. And even the pharaohs didn't go around killing people who only knew where the pyramid was located. Frankly, if I were capable of killing, don't you think I would have handled the supervisor myself? Why would I need a man from your agency?"

12

"Well," said the quiet man who still had not brought the glass to his lips.

"I see," said Van Riker. "You have been trained to be thorough beyond thorough, and you defend yourself as though others do the same. Like firing several shots instead of one. I heard you." Van Riker nodded thoughtfully and slowly took the glass of bourbon from the quiet man. He drank half of it.

"Okay?" he asked giving back the glass. "Not poisoned."

"Okay," said the quiet man, but when his glass was filled again, he did not drink until the General had first taken a drink from it.

"It's this whole thing," he explained apologetically. "It's been spooky since the beginning. From the bones on, it's been spooky. I mean it was bad enough having to live for so long with a man I was going to kill, but I can't tell you what those old bones did to us. Little babies! Those Indians must have been something, General."

He drank deeply and became mellow. He had not spoken to anyone for months.

General Van Riker listened, said that yes, the old Indians were indeed something, and suddenly snapped his fingers. "Oh, no. We forgot the seal. It's got to be sealed immediately. I was so upset over what you looked like—the blood and everything—I forgot about the seal. We've got to put it on right away. Come on."

The quiet man steadied himself against a small table He weaved a bit and tried to focus his eyes

13

better. It had been a long time since he had indulged himself.

"You know, General Van Riker, you're not real military, but I like you, buddy," he said, then poured himself another half-tumbler of bourbon and drank it down in one long gulp. "One for the prairie, heh, heh."

Van Riker smiled benignly and helped the man from the trailer.

"One more for my baby and one more for the prairie," sang the man who had been quiet for so long. "One more for my baby and one more for the road or prairie or missile site. One more for the pyramids. You know, Van Riker, I fucking love you, baby. Not queer love or anything. You know. You're the greatest fucking guy in the world."

Van Riker helped him up onto the giant marble base of the monument. "I'll lower the cap out of the truck," he said.

"Yeah. Fucking do that. Good idea. Lower the cap out of the truck." And the once quiet man began to sing a tuneless chant about lowering caps out of trucks all day and old man missile, he don't do nothing, just sits in his hole awaiting a button, old man missile, he just keeps waiting along.

"Hey, General, sweetheart, I'm a songwriter," he yelled, but he could not remember the lyrics, and besides, the metal arm extending from the truck over the plaque was sending out something. From the bottom it looked like a giant flattened barbell, and when it was over the two holes, he saw the two

14

round caps would fit exactly. A long wire lowered from one cap.

"Attach the wire to the bottom of one of the cylinders," yelled Van Riker.

"One of the cylinders is full."

"The empty one, then."

"Sure, old buddy." And in his revelry he grabbed the wire with both hands and jumped into the empty cylinder. The wire came with him, whirring from some sort of spool he could not see.

"There's a hook at your feet," yelled Van Riker. "You've got to tie the wire on."

"Looking for the hook, old boy, looking for the hook," sang the once quiet man to the tune of "Bringing in the Sheaves." Since there wasn't room to bend over, he had to squat and feel between his legs for the hook. The cylinder was black and cold against his cheek and back, skin-sticking cold.

When he finally got the wire wound around the hook, he heard something up above. It was the whirring sound from the spool. The wire stretched taut, pinning him against the cold metal side, and he saw the flattened dumbbell device coming down exactly over his hole, pulled by the very wire he had tied to the hook between his feet. He was sober in an instant.

He went for his gun to jam it between the cap and cylinder top, but by the time the gun was out of its holster, the cap had closed solidly and the stars above him were gone. He was in blackness now.

Up above, on the plain where Sioux war parties

and U.S. Cavalry had once massacred the helpless Apowas, General Douglas Van Riker climbed from the back of the van onto the marble monument.

It now had an airtight headstone sealing off the two bodies, hopefully forever. On the far side of the flattened dumbbell was the inscription, "Wounded Elk Massacre." On the near one was, "August 17, 1873."

The letters on the missile seal, the huge central bronze disk, read, "Here, on August 17, 1873, a unit of the United States Cavalry slaughtered fifty-five members of the Apowa Tribe. The Bureau of Indian Affairs and the nation deeply regret this crime and now, for all time, acknowledge its occurrence. February 23, 1961."

Van Riker read the inscription. More than a decade later he would be horrified by his choice camouflage. But at the time, he regarded it as so perfect that it was worth even the lives of the two men buried inside the marble monument beneath his feet.

Van Riker heard a muffled ping beneath him. The once quiet man was trying to shoot his way out. No matter. The bullet would probably spin around the burial cylinder until it stopped in the man. He was dead. If not now, minutes from now. If not by his own bullets, then by suffocation. It was unfortunate that anyone had to die, but this was not an ordinary missile. Two deaths now could save millions of lives later.

For this was a nuclear age, and the life of the entire planet might depend on the security precautions taken by men who controlled the nuclear weapons—of all nations. It was not a question of a better gun. It was a question of whether life would continue to exist on earth.

Van Riker had not worked so hard to design this installation for an ordinary missile. No, this missile was the Cassandra, and because it was the Cassandra, only one living man could know where it was and what it was. The supervisor had suspected this when he had begun to realize how this missile differed from others. So out went the quiet man with the drinking problem, who had been on the wagon for a long time. Even to this detail had Van Riker planned.

"I'm sorry, gentlemen," he said, knowing no one could hear him on the Montana prairie, "but there are millions whose lives will be saved by this. Maybe billions, because, gentlemen, this device should save us from a nuclear war." And then he thought of the layers of bodies he was standing on—bodies that had fallen there thousands of years before Christ and then in 1873 and now in 1961. Perhaps if the rest of the plan worked, there would never be another war, Van Riker thought.

He drove the truck along the dusty dirt road for about seventy miles before he saw human life—the small Apowa Indian reservation. He left the truck in a military parking field fifty miles farther east and without even checking to see if he had taken the keys from the ignition, he caught a commercial liner for the Bahamas, where he had an estate with very

17

efficient telephones connected directly to the Pentagon.

By the time Van Riker felt the first warmth of the Bahamas sun, a new air attaché was arriving at the United States Embassy in Moscow. He had a meeting scheduled in the Kremlin and had specified some of the men who must be there. He had named some scientists and military men and NKVD personnel, and—to the Russians' surprise—he named a man whose identity they had thought was secret, a man whom even most of the high-level NKVD foreign-bureau staffers did not know. Valashnikov.

Now, Valashnikov was twenty-eight years old—a good twenty years younger than all the other Russian military there, so young that in previous generations other officials would have assumed he was related to the czar. But in this generation, when they saw his smooth young face and the piercing black eyes of youth, they knew that here was probably a future chief of staff. Here was a genius. Here was a man who would, at the very least, command armies by the time he was their age. Command armies, if not the entire nation, although at this time he was only wearing the uniform of an NKVD colonel. So they were polite to Valashnikov, despite his youth and relatively low rank, for no one else in the room was less than a general.

"Gentlemen," said the American air attaché, "my government has asked to meet with you to explain a new development in missiles, a nuclear warhead."

The Russians nodded dully, all except the one

young man. He appeared more interested in cleaning his fingernails.

"It is essential for the effectiveness of the weapon that you know of its existence," the attaché continued.

"In that case, we are all leaving," said Colonel Valashnikov.

The older men looked at him, shocked. As they saw him go to the door, they too began to rise, because no one wanted to be the only person left in the room.

But Valashnikov stopped at the door, his pink cheeks beaming with the flush of victory. "So much for your weapon. We choose not to listen or believe and your weapon is nothing."

The men in the room saw the American smile weakly.

"But we are reasonable men," said Valashnikov. "If capitalists choose to spend their workers' wages on things which are nothing, we will be considerate." And Valashnikov returned to his seat at the table, as did all the others, realizing that Valashnikov had already won an important battle. The Americans would now have to tell them much more than they had intended if they wanted the Russians to believe it. And all this without even a threat. The boy colonel was a genius. A genius.

Those officers who did not know Valashnikov made it a point to look at him warmly and to smile during the meeting, which was now, of course, between the American general and the dashing young colonel.

"I am here to tell you about the Cassandra missile," said the American. And he told of a nuclear warhead made up of smaller warheads, some with their own projection devices. He talked about umbrella coverage and multiple reentry. Some Russians took notes. Others—those who had fought the great tank battles against the Nazis and did not know rocketry or nuclear warfare—listened with pretended understanding, grateful for men like Valashnikov, whose knowledge made it possible for them to ignore things like science and international politics.

"What you are describing is stupid," said Valashnikov. "That is the dirtiest nuclear warhead I have ever heard of. It is irresponsible in the extreme. It would have, at best, only vague accuracy. You would barely hit our continent with it. After you've fired it, don't expect to be eating fish from the sea for the next five generations. If there *are* five generations. Absurd!"

"Thank you," said the American general coolly. "Thank you for understanding the Cassandra. It will only be fired if you should attack first and succeed. In other words, you now know that if we lose a nuclear war, you've lost, also."

"Idiot!" shouted Valashnikov. "I rejected a similar device two years ago, before it got off the drawing board. It's unstable, you fool. Even in the ground it's unstable."

But the American general was not listening to him. He was headed toward the door, with a blank smile on his face. It was his turn not to listen.

When the American was gone, Valashnikov's anger vanished and he gave a little shrug. To the chief of staff he explained that the way to handle the Cassandra was to find it and leave it where it was. "You see," he explained to the field marshal, "the weakness of the Cassandra is partly psychological, which is also its strength. Let me explain. If you believe no one will dare attack you, you become lax. If you believe you have the perfect defense, then you began wasting your money on such things as social improvements and the like. Now if we find where it is, then ignore it, we leave them their illusion. Until we decide to attack. And of course our first strike in an attack is the Cassandra."

"What if they have two Cassandras? Even three?" asked the field marshal who had begun his military career with a saber and now saw himself ending it as a scientific philosopher.

Valashnikov shook his head. "It's technical, and I think our scientists would bear me out. You are not going to have two Cassandras or three. Because if two or three should go, it could—in the simplest sense—create a planetwide Dresden effect."

"You mean the bombing in World War II where the very air burned, it was so hot?"

"Correct," said Valashnikov. "Only here it would literally have the oxygen feeding a nuclear fire so hot and so consuming that conceivably all oxygen would be burned from the planet. All life. No. Two or three Cassandras goes beyond irresponsibility into insanity. Insane the Americans are not."

"Don't be so sure," said the adviser on interna-

21

tional relations. "Look at what they just did in Cuba."

Everyone laughed. It was a good tension breaker.

To the NKVD chief and to the chief of the foreign bureau Valashnikov explained that the Cassandra would not be all that difficult to find. At least five feet of it had to be above ground and encased, probably in marble or at least some form of rock material. Also, the Cassandra had another drawback that would be most noticeable.

"Bronze," said one of the scientists, smiling. "Of course. Bronze. A shield of bronze twenty feet in diameter. Removable for firing."

Valashnikov nodded. And imitating the American, he said, "Gentlemen, we have a great problem ahead of us. We must find a giant piece of marble with a bronze center, far away from any American population center. And in case we don't recognize it instantly, the center has to be perfectly round. A real problem, gentlemen. It should take us days, at least, gentlemen."

Everyone laughed except the field marshal. "How days?" he asked. He had seen many things go wrong, from cavalary charges to the new tank the Germans were supposed to be so afraid of that they would never attack. He still had scars from when he had escaped from the flaming turret of one of those tanks in June 1941.

"Well, for one thing, Comrade Field Marshal, we have our own observation satellites, and they can pick up marble and bronze with ease."

"Statues are made of marble and bronze," said

the field marshal. "And there are many statues in America."

"Yes, there are, comrade, and someone who has served with the czar would be well aware of statues and the like. And so is the NKVD. I don't think we are going to miss a marble and bronze configuration of the likes that hides the Cassandra in some desert somewhere. Besides, its construction must have taken many workers many months. Our agents will know of it."

"What if it is not in desert? What if it is in city?"

"I doubt they would put something as unstable as the Cassandra in a city, Comrade Field Marshal. They could not keep secret the labors of so many workers for so long."

"I remember Americans," said the field marshal. "All the impossible things they did. Oh, yes, everybody laughs at them today, but I tell you, those soft, silly self-indulgent children become very tough and shrewd when they have to. Oh, yes. I know what you think. You think, there is field marshal who started out as sergeant in czar's cavalry. There is field marshal who brought hot chocolate to Stalin and survived and became general. There is field marshal who fought Germans with tanks and then befriended both Beria and Khruschev and became field marshal. Well, I tell you men of slide rules, I have seen Russian blood spilled by Russians. I have seen Russian blood spilled by Germans. I have seen Russian blood spilled by Chinese and Americans and by Englishmen and Finns."

Tears were welling up in the strong swollen face

of the field marshal, and some of the scientists were becoming a bit embarrassed.

"I will see no more Russian blood spilled than I have to. I have seen enough. You, Valashnikov, young man of such confidence and assurance, you who have never cried and prayed to God . . . yes, prayed to God . . . I have seen even political commissars do it during the hard winters of the last war . . . You, who think that all things can be worked out in mind and on paper . . . You, before you do another thing, find that Cassandra missile. Find it. You will do nothing else, rise to no other rank, until you find that horror for Mother Russia. I say, Mother Russia. Mother Russia. Mother Russia. Good day, gentlemen. God bless Mother Russia."

After the field marshal left, there was silence in the room, embarrassed silence. Finally Valashnikov spoke. "He's fallen right into their psychological trap. And to think we beat the Germans with that. Well, I don't see this taking any more than a week. Any of you see it differently?"

None did that day. But as the week passed and then the month and then many months, many of the top officers began remembering that, like the field marshal, they too, had thought the Cassandra might pose some problems.

And Valashnikov watched his classmates become captains, then majors, then lieutenant colonels and colonels, while he still searched for the Cassandra. One day he thought he had found it, but that turned out to be his most bitter disappointment. Everything was perfect for the Cassandra, but the marble and

24

bronze turned out to be a stupid monument to some dead savages, much like the Russians' own Tartars. It was on that day that Valashnikov noticed the first hint of a receding hairline and realized that he was not a young man any more. And he was still a colonel.

Time passed in America, also. And what was once considered a noble monument constructed by the Bureau of Indian Affairs had become a rallying point for what many perceived as a grievous injustice to the only indigenous Americans. Especially after the best-selling book by Lynn Cosgrove, *My Soul Rises from Wounded Elk*.

Shouting, "It is a good day to die," some forty men and women wearing Indian warpaint and bonnets had seized the marble and bronze monument out in the Montana prairie and the Episcopal church that had been built a few yards from it. They wanted to bring attention, their leaders said, "to the oppression of the American Indian."

Real Apowa Indians—who had in the past ten years moved from their reservation and built the town of Wounded Elk half a mile from the monument—watched the goings-on and scratched their heads.

Television cameras came in to surround Wounded Elk. Federal marshals moved in and formed a giant loose circle around the monument and the Episcopal church but made no effort to remove the Indians. And General Van Riker was watching on Bahamian television as half a dozen of the Indians banged away with rifle butts on the bronze shield of the Cassandra. Then some lunatic began working with a power drill. General Van Riker phoned the Pentagon and demanded to speak to the chairman of the Joint Chiefs of Staff.

A snotty brigadier explained to Van Riker that he had clearance only for a Max-Emergency 7 call, which did not exist except in case of nuclear war.

"Put on the admiral," said Van Riker, "or you'll end your career in Leavenworth, making little ones out of big ones."

"Yes," came the admiral's somnolent tones from the receiver. "What do you want, Van Riker?"

"We've got a problem."

"Can we talk about it Monday?"

"There may not be a Monday," said Van Riker. "Not for us, at least . . ."

CHAPTER TWO

His name was Remo, and he had a problem. With-out breaking any possible instruments, he had to snatch someone named Douglas Van Riker, fifty-six, Caucasian, tan, with gleaming white hair, blue eyes, and a mole under his left arm. Which was only the first part of the problem.

"Are you Douglas Van Riker?" asked Remo of a white-haired, blue-eyed gentleman with a fine, rich tan, reading *Fortune* magazine in the Bahamian Air-port. The man wore an expensive white silk suit that seemed to match his perfect smile. Even if he hadn't been reading *Fortune,* he looked as if he could have been in it.

"No. Sorry, I'm not, old boy," said the man pleasantly.

Remo grabbed the left side of the man's white silk suit and, gripping a handful of nylon shirt with it, ripped it off the man in one wrenching tear. He checked the armpit. There was no mole.

"Right you are," Remo said. "You're right. I have to admit it. I'll admit that. You're right. No mole."

27

The man blinked, mouth agape, suit half off, magazine dangling.

"Wha?" he said, stunned.

"What are you doing half-dressed, George?" asked a portly woman sitting next to him.

"A man came over to me, asked me if I were Douglas Van Riker, and ripped off my suit. I've never seen hands move so fast."

"Why would he rip your suit off, dear, if you're not this Douglas person?"

"Why would he rip it off even if I were? Look. There he goes," said the half-dressed man. He pointed to a man about six feet tall, lean and wiry, with high cheekbones and surprisingly large wrists. The man wore gray slacks and a blue sports shirt.

"Someone's pointing at you, sir," the young man was told by a man with hair so white it looked bleached. "Odd. He seems half-undressed."

"Don't mind him," said Remo. "Are you Douglas Van Riker?"

"Why do you want to know?"

"Don't be rude. I asked first," Remo said.

"Turn around and you'll see that the man who was pointing at you is now approaching with two constables."

"I don't have time to be bothered," said Remo. "Are you Douglas Van Riker?"

"Yes, I am, and when you get out of jail, look me up."

Remo felt a hand on his shoulder. Grabbing its palm, he snapped it forward to see who was attached. It was a constable. The constable went back-crack-ing into a reservation booth. The second hand that touched him also belonged to a constable. He sailed into a baggage turntable and kept spinning slowly, along with the luggage of incoming Pan Am flight 105 from O'Hare.

"My God," said Van Riker. "I've never seen hands so fast. You didn't even turn around."

"That's not fast. Fast is when you don't see them," said Remo. "C'mon, we've got work to do. You are Douglas Van Riker."

"Yes, I am, and I like to stay dressed."

"Do you have any baggage?"

"Just this grip?"

Remo checked the name tag. It said Van Riker. The white-haired man offered his wallet. There were credit cards, driver's license, and military identification. He was a lieutenant general, United States Air Force, retired.

"Good," said Remo. "Come with me. That flight's going to Washington. You don't want that."

"I do want that."

"No, you don't. You want to go with me. Don't make a scene. I can't stand scenes."

"But I will make a scene," said Van Riker. Suddenly he felt an incredible wrenching pain in his right ribs.

"Now, *that* was fast," Remo said. C'mon. people are looking."

Doing his best to keep his weight off his right side and trying not to breathe deeply, Van Riker went with the young man to a cab outside. They drove to a small private airfield, where Van Riker saw a black Lear Jet, prepped for takeoff.

29

"Where are we going?" asked Van Riker as he was being helped up the small platform ladder that was the entrance to the jet.

"For you to get some answers."

When the plane was airborne, Van Riker asked for a painkiller for his rib. But instead of chemicals, he got the young man reaching around to his spinal column. Then there was a little tap, and then, blessedly, the rib no longer hurt.

"Nerves," said Remo. "Your rib wasn't cracked. It was the nerves."

"Thank you. Could you explain yourself a little more clearly? Where are we going? Who are you? Why have you kidnapped me?"

"Not kidnapped," Remo said. "I'm borrowing you. I think we're on the same side."

"I'm not on any side," said Van Riker. "I'm retired. I was an administrative officer in the United States Air Force. Would you care to know how many towels we had at Lackland?"

"I didn't break any instruments, did I?"

"Of course not," Van Riker said. "I'm not carrying instruments. Why would I carry instruments?"

"I haven't the foggiest. I just follow orders," said Remo. "You're going to talk to someone you're going to like."

"I don't think I'm going to like anyone, being kidnapped like this. Is it money you want? Do you want money? I can guarantee a reasonable amount of money if you cooperate."

"I've got enough," Remo said.

"I'll pay you more."

"How can you pay more than enough?" asked Remo. "That's not logical. And they say you're a big-ass scientist. God save America."

"If you believe in America, get me to Washington. It's urgent."

"You're not going to Washington. Shut up," Remo said.

"God save America," said Van Riker. And there was silence until the plane landed at a small private field, which Remo explained was just outside Goldsboro, North Carolina, site of a large air force base.

As soon as General Van Riker had his feet on the ground behind the younger man, the plane began taxiing back down the runway.

"Where is he going?"

"Away from here. Smitty doesn't like to let anyone know what he's doing. He's the guy you're going to see. A bit peculiar, but okay."

"If you think someone is peculiar," said General Van Riker, "God help us. God help him."

"You're pretty religious for a scientist who invented one pisser of a missile," said Remo.

Hearing that was more shocking than the sudden pain in the ribs had been. Years of training for such a moment had barely prevented Van Riker from gasping in disbelief.

It was impossible for this man to know about the bomb. Impossible. The whole thing had been designed so that no one would know about it except Van Riker, the president, and the chairman of the Joint Chiefs of Staff. And all the chairman knew was that there was a weapon. Not what kind and not

31

where. That was the strength of the Cassandra. That no one but Van Riker knew where it was. For if the other side ever found out, it could detonate it without all that much difficulty. A ground-level explosion with the Dresden effect climbing instead of descending.

As Van Riker followed the young man into a hangar, he thought he heard something. He was deeply shaken. "Are you whistling?" he asked incredulously.

"Yeah."

"Merrily whistling?"

"Yeah."

"Do you know that at any moment you might be a cinder?"

"So?"

"So why are you so damned happy with yourself?"

"I did my job. You're here. With no broken instruments."

"Doesn't it bother you that you could be burned alive in a nuclear holocaust?"

"As opposed to a bullet in the brain or what? Nuclear holocaust doesn't grab me. You know I could kill myself by incorrect balance during some of my thrusts? Did you know that? How would you like to die just because your technique is wrong? That's awful. That's frightening. Incorrect technique gives me nightmares."

At the far end of the hangar was a man in dark suit and tie. He sat behind a small desk, reading. To the right was a frail wisp of an Oriental with a thin, straggly white beard. He wore a red and gold robe, and sat in lotus position atop a large, brightly lacquered steamer trunk. There were thirteen others nearby.

"Down at the far end is Smitty," said Remo, pointing to the man at the desk.

Walking toward the figure at the far end of the hangar, Van Riker heard his captor say to the old Oriental, "You know, Little Father, that guy doesn't give a second thought to technique. Invents a bomb that can wipe out a continent and poison the world, and he doesn't give a faded fart about technique."

"When a person cannot do one thing well, he seeks to do many to compensate. Then, in the confusion, he hopes no one will notice his unworthiness. If this one could have made a bomb to kill one person correctly, then he would have done something worthwhile. But he could not. So he made a bomb to kill a lot of persons badly. He is a menace to himself and to those around him," said the Oriental.

"He's an American air force general, Little Father."

"Oh," said the Oriental, as if that statement explained everything. "The surpreme example of quantity triumphant over quality."

Van Riker heard the last remark, but it did not bother him. The disaster he had dreamed of at night and wrestled with beneath consciousness during waking hours was happening now. And he, the only man who might avert the holocaust, was the captive of lunatics. It was almost a blessed relief to see the very conservative suit and the dry lemony face of the man who introduced himself as Dr. Harold W. Smith.

"Please sit down," said Smith. "I know you must be in great torment. We are here to help you do what you must do. And there is no one else as capable as we are of helping you. Ordinarily, we would not be involved in a mission of this sort. But we know about Cassandra. We know it's at Wounded Elk."

"What is this about?" asked Van Riker. "I'm on my way to a vacation in Washington. I am kidnapped and then told of some wounded animal and a character from Greek poetry and some horrible missile . . . I just don't understand."

"Precisely," said Smith. "Precisely. Why should you trust us? And that's my job now. I propose, General Van Riker, creator of the Cassandra missile, that you let us help you do what you must do."

"My God, this is a nightmare! Who are you? I never had anything to do with missiles. I was a logistics officer."

"And so your cover says," Smith said. "And so too do many things. What I propose now is to use your mind to prove to you that we are both on the same side and that we are the only people who can help you do what you must do about the Cassandra. One: we are not foreign. If we were foreign, just knowing for certain the whereabouts of Cassandra would be all we need. It's a vulnerable, unstable weapon whose main protection is its camouflage. Because it could be triggered in its silo, once known to a foreign power, it's more a danger to the United States than to anyone else. Correct?"

Van Riker denied nothing. His face was stone, but he was listening.

"Two: are we some sort of criminal organization that could effectively blackmail the United States by threatening to trigger the Cassandra? A very effective blackmail, I might add. To answer this, I am going to have to disclose to you something so critical to the functioning of America that I have ordered people killed who knew about it. When you know who we are, you will realize that we are probably the only people who could know about Cassandra, outside of yourself. And when I tell you who we are, you will know I have given you a greater weapon against us than any we have against you."

"Do you have a cigarette?" asked Van Riker. He felt hot, and his body ached for air or nicotine or something.

"No. I'm sorry. I don't smoke."

"I gave it up a few years ago," said Van Riker. "Go on."

Van Riker felt weak, even sitting down. Smith offered him water, and he took it, then listened as Smith explained.

More than a decade before, it had become obvious to the president in power that America was headed toward becoming a police state. The cause was chaos—not just mobs taking over the streets but corporations acting like self-governments with no respect for law, transportation virtually owned by racketeers, corruption emerging in every facet of American life.

"It is a law of history that chaos brings dictatorship," Smith said. "But the president thought that America was too good to give up, that maybe there was another way, and he decided that all the Constitution needed was a little assist. Unbribe a judge here, protect a witness there, that sort of thing."

"What you're saying is that the Constitution couldn't work without its being violated," said Van Riker. "To get away with that, you'd have to keep your system entirely clean of informers. Exposure is the one thing you couldn't stand."

"Exactly," said Smith. "You're really quite brilliant. To guard against exposure, we had to have a killer arm."

Van Riker took a notebook from his pocket and began doodling. "I'd figure eight hundred men."

"That would be impossible, and you know it," said Smith. "You're an expert on security. You know five people cannot keep a secret. So we have only three who know. Myself, Remo, whom you met, and each president . . ."

"Is there a control on the president?" asked Van Riker.

"Of course. He can only disband us. He cannot order us," Simth said.

"I imagine you've done extensive work in job-separation function."

"Of course," Smith said. "It's basically an isolation function worked off a simple computer program. Only way you can employ people without letting them know the nature of the operation. Large numbers, of course. In addition . . ."

At the entrance to the hangar, extrasensitive ears

picked up the mounting excitement tinged with joy in the voices of Van Riker and Smith.

"I told you, Little Father," Remo said, "that those two whackos would get along fine. Sounds like two kids with their model boats. 'Job-separation function.' What the hell are they talking about?"

"It has been a thought in the House of Sinanju for hundreds of years," said Chiun, the master of Sinanju, "that royalty marries royalty not so much because it is a powerful alliance but because only royalty can comprehend royalty. Or tolerate it, for that matter."

"I don't understand, Little Father," said Remo. Since his training had begun, more than a decade before, he had come to understand occasionally, without explanation, some of the wisdom of the House of Sinanju, an ages-old house of Korean assassins, of which Chiun was the master.

"Whom do you like to talk to most of all?" asked Chiun.

"Why, I guess, you, because we do the same work." Chiun nodded.

"And I guess that you like, most of all, talking to me," said Remo, smiling.

Chiun shook his head. "What I like most of all is me." See? I am royalty . . . the master."

"I know that. I meant after that," said Remo, kicking a piece of the wood flooring out the hangar entrance. "Ding dong dink," he muttered.

Back at the table Van Riker was watching an organization unfold before his eyes.

"The bottom line," said Smith, "is that we don't think the military is capable of handling this situation properly—especially since it's worse than you might think."

"I don't see how it could be."

"When you built Cassandra, in 1961, we had nuclear superiority over the Russians. We don't anymore. We didn't really need Cassandra then. It was just extra insurance. But we do need it now. With its strategic advantage, Russia would attack in a moment if it thought it could eliminate the Cassandra. And as you well know, if the joint chiefs attempt to protect it, they'll do it with a division, and the whole world will know where it is. The Cassandra is much like my agency, CURE. If we're known, we fail."

"What can you give me?" asked Van Riker.

"The finest killers in the world."

"How many?"

"Both of them," said Smith nodding to the hangar entrance.

"The Oriental looks barely ambulatory."

"He's number one," said Smith.

"I guess they're your enforcement arm. Your eight hundred men rolled into two."

"Rolled into one," said Smith. "Remo is the enforcement arm. Chiun is his trainer and seems to go along to protect his investment of training, as far as I can gather. One does not press the master of Sinanju for what he regards as petty details."

"A one-man killer arm," mused Van Riker. "Probably had a lot of assignments. Friends and acquaintances . . . even family around the country. Fingerprints. Let me guess . . . Are you using a dead man?"

"Remo Williams, a Newark policeman, was executed more than a decade ago. The fingerprints of this orphan are no longer on file anywhere," said Smith.

"A man who doesn't exist for an organization that doesn't exist," said Van Riker, nodding with respect.

Smith smiled. "If I ever have a successor, I hope he is just like you. You're correct one hundred percent."

"And now I am the fourth man to know," said Van Riker. "Because you want . . ."

"Because we need to trust each other," said Smith. "Because . . ."

"Because there won't be a country to defend unless we secretly safeguard the Cassandra," said Van Riker.

He stood up and offered his hand. Smith rose and accepted it.

"Done," they said in unison, and Smith walked Van Riker to the hanger entrance, an arm about the general's shoulder.

"Good luck," said Smith. "If you have to reach me, call the Folcroft Sanitarium, in Rye, New York."

"That's your cover?"

"Right. I'm director of the sanitarium. The sanitarium line is an open line. The closed lines are a variation code off a multiple of five, based on the day of the week, Greenwich mean time."

"Convenient," said Van Riker.

"Gibberish," said Remo.

"You put up with that?" asked Van Riker.

"Have to. He's the best in the business."

Chiun whispered to Remo. "How would he know?"

"He counts the bodies, Little Father."

"That's so white of him," said Chiun.

Van Riker had one more question. How did Smith find out about the Cassandra?

"That, sir," said Smith, "you know if you think about it." Remo thought he saw the first beam of joy ever to emanate from Smith's face.

"Of course," said Van Riker. "I was singular-oriented, and you, by your very nature, are multiple."

"What does that mean?" Remo asked.

"It means, basically," said Van Riker, "that Cassandra was set up against Russian detection, and even our own military detection, but not against an organization that had perceptors out in every government agency and could reduce data in a simple job-program function. It was inevitable that you would know about it by what you didn't get in feedback."

"A negative positive," said Smith.

"Of course," said Van Riker.

"Of course," said Chiun.

Remo looked at him quizzically.

"Let me handle this one, my son. He might prove some trouble," said Chiun in basic Korean.

"I still don't understand," Remo told Van Riker.

There was a new jet waiting with a new pilot. Over Arkansas, Van Riker explained to Remo how CURE had discovered Cassandra. What it sounded like he said was that many people reporting on materials and people movement could be simplified in computers to show what they were doing just by what they pretended not to be doing.

"I still don't understand," said Remo.

"You don't have to," said Van Riker.

40

"Pay attention," said Chiun to Remo. "You might learn something." And behind Van Riker's back he gave Remo a big wink, then rolled his eyes back in his head, indicating that he thought the white-haired man was a lunatic.

Over Wounded Elk the plane shuddered. Van Riker's tan whitened. In a few moments he said shakily, "Thank God. It was only an air pocket."

CHAPTER THREE

The plan Smith had outlined was simple in concept. First, protect the bronze nuclear cap under the monument so that midwestern America did not become a cinder. Then make sure to protect the continuing secrecy of the Cassandra, whose exposure could set up a dangerous nuclear imbalance.

But there was a flaw in the plan.

The flaw was ABC, CBS, NBC, the *New York Times*, the *New York Globe*, the *Washington Post*, the *San Francisco Chronicle*, the *Chicago Tribune*, the *London Daily Mail*, *Time*, *Newsweek*, *Esquire*, *Paris-Match*, the *Asahi Shimbun*, United Press International, Associated Press, Reuters, Pravda, and several hundred other representatives of the media, all stretched out like an undulating picket line along the flat Montana prairie, made dust-brown by a hot summer and a long drought.

Half a mile away, atop a flat mesa, was the town of Wounded Elk. It had been set up ten years before by Apowa tribesmen who had left the reservation, trudged along the now paved road, and began to build the good life for themselves. However, the press of the world was not interested in the two thousand Indians who lived in the town. They were interested instead in the forty Indians from Chicago, Harlem, Hollywood, and Harvard, who had seized the monument and the church along the paved road leading to the new town of Wounded Elk.

Federal marshals still formed a large loose ring around the Indian invaders, but they were under orders from Washington not to try to evict the protestors, lest anyone think it was a repressive act. At first the marshals had tried to keep the press away from the protesters, but it had turned out to be too much work and now they weren't trying too hard.

As Remo watched, he saw a blue flag being carried by someone from the church to the monument. The cameramen readied themselves. The man dropped the flag, raised a Russian Kalashnikov rifle above his head, jumped onto the marble monument, he did a war dance then jumped back down.

"We didn't get that one. We didn't get that one," Remo heard one cameraman say. "Wave to them or something."

There was waving from the front line of the newsmen, and then a voice bellowed through a megaphone from near the monument, "Whatsa matter with you shits? You had the blue flag on that one."

"Some of us missed it, sir," yelled back one reporter.

"All right," bellowed the voice. "But this is it. No more for today."

The man with braided black hair again jumped up on top of the marble monument, did his war dance,

43

waving his rifle, then jumped back down and strolled back to the church.

The cameraman then turned his camera to his announcer, who began to intone what sounded like a conclusion to a television news show.

"So, surrounded by armed federal marshals, the Revolutionary Indian Party vows to fight to the death or until, as they say, full and just rights are returned to their people. This is . . ."

The announcer was interrupted by a young blonde girl wearing Indian beads and screaming, "The whole world is watching! The whole world is watching! The whole world is watching!"

Remo grabbed the hysterical girl by the arm and dragged her off to the edge of the crowd, where federal marshals had cordoned off a huge parking lot for the media. Twice the size of a football field, the area was so tangled with electrical cords from the television vans that it looked like a field of black spaghetti.

"Where are you taking me, you bastard?" yelled the girl. "Oppressive male chauvinist pig."

"I want you to do something for me."

"Pig bastard."

"Please don't yell. The whole world is watching," said Remo as they approached a black limousine.

"The whole world is watching. The whole world is watching!" shrieked the girl vengefully. "The whole word is watching!"

With one hand Remo opened the rear door of the car, and with the other, he shoved the shrieking head into the back seat.

"The whole world is watching! The whole world is watching!" the girl continued. Remo held her up to Van Riker's face, and when the general nodded that he had had enough, Remo threw the girl, spinning, several cars away. She cracked into a hood ornament and was quiet.

"That," said Remo, "is the minor flaw in your plan. It is very hard to be inconspicuous when the whole world is watching."

"Hmmmm," said Van Riker.

"Any other bright ideas?"

"The very negativeness of it is positive," said Chiun, and only Remo knew he was ridiculing.

"Of course," said Van Riker. "But how do we use it?"

"Look," said Remo, "I will stay at the monument and protect the shield. You go do what you want to do. Maybe you and Smitty can play code or something. Chiun will stay with you."

"What are you going to do? How are you going to do it?"

"You're the greatest single disaster to hit this country since the Civil War, and you're asking *me* my plans. My plan is this: try to undo some of the disaster out there. How does that sound?"

"Don't get snotty with me, son. The only reason I want you is that a division of armor would give us away. There is some delicacy involved in this thing. We need secrecy."

"We're not exactly a public organization, either, Van Riker," said Remo.

"Let me speak to him," Chiun said to Van Riker. "I will teach him respect for authority."

Chiun left the car with Remo, and once they were away from Van Riker's hearing, asked if it were true that America faced a holocaust of fire. Remo said this was what Smith had said and Van Riker had verified.

"And is it true that America would be but a shell of a country if this happened?"

"Probably, Little Father."

"Then our course is clear. We must seek employment elsewhere. Persia during the summer, my son, is a most delicious place for an assassin. There is a melon that ripens just before dawn . . ."

"Forget it. I'm not going," said Remo, and he headed toward the first ring of newsmen with Chiun's recriminations in his ears. He knew the whole speech by heart: how Chiun had found an inadequate piece of a pale pig's ear and given it the wisdom of the House of Sinanju and how this ingrate cast aside this great wisdom and risked his life wantonly in the service of foolish causes—this, after the master of Sinanju had devoted some of the best years of his life to Remo's training. Was Remo aware how much of the master's time would have been wasted if his pupil got himself killed? And for what? A two-hundred-year-old country? The House of Sinanju was ages older than that, but then again, being white, Remo probably could not count very well, either.

Chiun returned to Van Riker's car, mumbling. Within twenty-five feet two networks and a newspaper approached him for interviews, asking if he were someone.

"Are you supporting Third World liberation, sir?" asked a deep-voice newsman. Chiun saw the camera. He saw the makeup on the man's face.

"Third World is what?" asked the master of Sinanju.

"All browns, blacks, yellows, and Latin Americans."

"Yes, I support totally Third World liberation—with some minor exceptions, which include browns, blacks, Latins, the Chinese, Thais, Japanese, Filipinos, Burmese and Vietnamese."

"That doesn't leave too much, sir."

"That leaves all one needs. That leaves the Koreans," said Chiun, raising a wizened hand with long fingernails. And lest the newsman spread improper thoughts, he explained that not even all Koreans were worthy of liberations. The southerners were lazy, and Yalu villages were dirty, and Pyong Yang was really a whorehouse in disguise. But the village of Sinanju—that was worthy of liberation, except of course the four houses by the bay, the fishermen's wharf, the weaver's house. And naturally, one would not consider the farmers part of the village, since they never raised enough to feed anyone, anyhow.

"What do you like about the Third World then?"

"No whites," said Chiun.

Seeing the Oriental giving an interview, another television reporter joined in to ask him what was going to happen at Wounded Elk, where the Indian movement was going, and how the government could best relate to the Indians.

Since everyone liked money, Chiun said, the government ought to give the Indians more money, under the assumption that if the government gave them dried fish, they might not like it. Chiun had found through bitter experience that many people didn't like dried fish, especially Westerners. So money was nicer.

This was immediately translated to national television as a "nonnegotiable demand by a militant Third World spokesman."

"Will you fight to the earth, sir?"

"Yours, yes—mine, no," said Chiun, summing up the essence of Sinanju training.

The newspaper reporter was with a photographer, and when Chiun entered the car with Van Riker, his picture was taken, Van Riker tried to shield his face, and that was a mistake, because it triggered a flurry of shots as he drove away angrily over television cables and past federal marshals, mumbling to the Oriental, who seemed incredibly placid.

"Do your instruments need protection?" asked Chiun.

"No. I don't have them with me," said Van Riker. "We're going to them."

Van Riker parked the car at a nearby highway motel that looked as if it were made of beaverboard and staples. He did not bother going to the office but went directly to a tacky room door and opened it with a key from his pocket. He saw the Oriental shuffle to an Apowa Indian in dungarees, leaning against the office door. The Apowa followed the

48

Oriental to the car and removed the one trunk the Oriental had brought with him.

Inside the room the Oriental told the Apowa that "the young man" would take care of it, and Van Riker tipped the Indian a dollar, then nodded him out of the room.

From a closet Van Riker took a cleaning man's gray uniform and a brush with a long handle that looked something like a broom.

"These are all I need," said Van Riker. "I'll need room, however, to work on some diagrams.

Chiun heard the remark, thought a moment, and then realized the white man could not mean what he said. So he ignored him.

Van Riker was amazed at how quickly the old Oriental had arranged the room. Where Van Riker wanted his map and diagram of Wounded Elk and the wiring charts of the monument, the Oriental had a television set rigged with a taping device so that, Van Riker could tell, the set was taping two other channels while the Oriental was watching the third.

"Excuse me," said Van Riker, "I do not wish to be insulting, but the future of the United States depends on the accuracy of my calculations. I would very much appreciate your moving your television set so that I could set up my charts."

"Use the bathroom," said Chiun.

"I don't think you realize how vitally important this is."

"This is the second time you have interrupted my daytime dramas of beauty. Most do not survive the

49

first. But let it not be said that the House of Sinanju is not willing to sacrifice to a larger good."

"Thank you," said Van Riker.

"You may live," said Chiun. "Go to the bathroom and save your country."

Meanwhile, Remo was approaching the line of federal marshals. They waved him back, but he continued on. One marshal raised a rifle to his shoulder and threatened to shoot. Remo saw the safety was on and continued up to the line.

"Where are you going, buddy?" asked one marshal, a chubby oily-faced man with a pencil mustache.

Remo clapped his on the marshal's shoulder in an affectionate display of camaraderie. "I'm one of you," said Remo, sliding his hand off the man's shoulder. "Just been assigned here from Washington to check things out. Keep up the good work."

Remo walked away from the man and casually pocketed the badge he had taken from the man's breast pocket. He flashed it at another marshal a hundred yards down, passed through the line, and started walking toward the church and monument.

As he approached a trench beside the road that passed the monument and church, a woman in deerskin with surprisingly white skin for an Indian rose from the trench. She pointed a pistol at Remo's belly.

"Who are you?" she demanded.

"George Armstrong Custer," said Remo, who saw that the safety was on.

"You're now a prisoner of the Revolutionary Indian Party, Mr. Custer."

"C'mon, c'mon, I got a deal for your leader. My name's Remo."

She ushered him past the trench toward the church. Two men were sitting on the church steps, playing pinochle, shotguns resting in their laps, passing a bottle of Corby's Whiskey back and forth between them.

As far as Remo could tell, one owed the other $23.50 and would pay it just as soon as they liberated another town from white oppression.

They looked up as Remo and the woman approached.

"One of the reporters sneaking through. And without our summoning him," said the woman.

"Well, leave him here and get the hell out. And what's for dinner?" asked one of the men with a meld.

"You can't talk to me like that. This is the liberation movement. I'm sharing your struggle to free our people from oppression."

"My apologies, comrade. What's for super, ms.?"

"Buffalo."

"Buffalo? There are no buffalo here."

"The new buffalo," said the young woman.

"You mean the cow behind the church?"

"The cow and all the other buffalo—the buffalo that roam department stores resting on our land, the buffalo that fill the supermarkets with food grown on our land, and the buffalo in the jewelry stores full of jewels purchased with what was stolen from us. Our buffalo. We are a race of hunters."

"They're still shooting the cow," said the man, melding a flush and a hundred aces and rewarding himself with another long draft from the bottle.

"It will be dead by supper, at least," said the girl.

"Then it has to be skinned."

"Then we must liberate the food from the stores," she said.

"The only stores are up in the Apowa village," the man said, taking a trick. "I don't think they'd like us liberating their food."

"Our food, our food," the girl shrieked shrilly. "It's not their food. It's our food. Our blood has bought this land for us."

"Yeah, yeah, yeah, yeah," said the man. "Shuffle."

"Take me to your leader," said Remo. "I wish to support his valiant struggle against oppressive white racism. I want to be one of you. I am one of you. I am Indian."

"I've never seen you in Chicago," said the man looking up. "Where do you live in Chicago?"

"Since when do you have to be from Chicago to join the Revolutionary Indian Party?" asked Remo.

"You don't. Not technically. It's just that with all our members in Chicago, we don't have to spend a lot of money on mailing things around the country. I'll tell you what. You can give us moral support. How much moral support you got in your pockets?"

"Couple of hundred," said Remo and threw some bills on the steps.

"I accept your support, brother. Now get the hell

out of here. You like Indians? Go visit the Apowa village."

"I know where you can get food. Luscious sirloins and fried chicken, crisp on the outside and oozy-juicy tender on the inside," Remo said.

"Don't weaken, brothers. We will hunt the buffalo and be free," the woman said.

"Strawberry ice cream on blueberry pie, hot pastrami and lager beer, sausage pizza and roast stuffed goose," Remo continued.

"He lies. The truth is not in him," said the girl.

"Shut up, Cosgrove," said the man. "You want to see Dennis Petty, right?"

"If he's the leader, yes," said Remo.

"When does the food come?"

"I can get it to you tonight."

"I haven't had a good lasagna since I don't know when. Could you get lasagna? I mean, not the packaged crap the Episcopalians are shipping in, but really good lasagne."

"Lasagne like your mother made?"

"My mother didn't make lasagne. She was half-Catawba and half-Irish."

"But her soul was all Catawba," said the girl named Cosgrove.

"Shut up, Cosgrove."

"Is that Lynn Cosgrove, who wrote *My Soul Rises from Wounded Elk?*" asked Remo.

"And as unwrapped as confetti," said the man.

"I am not Lynn Cosgrove. I am Burning Star."

"She's really buggy on this," said the man, putting

53

down his pinochle hand. "I'm Jerry Lupin. This is Bart Thompson."

"They're Wild Pony and Running Bear," said Burning Star.

"Didn't I see her somewhere?" Remo asked Lupin.

"Yeah. The Academy Awards. Ruined the whole show. Debbie Reynolds was supposed to sing. And this one had to get her rocks off about RIP. It's nuts like her that ruin everything. C'mon, I'll take you to Petty."

"He's in war council. Do not let the white oppressor into our sacred councils of war," cried Burning Star.

"Cosgrove," said Lupin, making a fist. "You shut your mouth or you'll be wearing pontoons for a smile."

Remo saw her raise the large pistol shakily and point it at his head.

"I will see tomorrow free or I will bathe this sacred soil in white blood. White blood is the only blood that can cleanse this continent. Rivers of white blood. Oceans of white blood," chanted Burning Star.

Remo slapped the gun away, and Burning Star blinked in amazement, then covered her face and cried.

"She always gets like that after a food delivery from the Episcopalians," Lupin said. "They send it in on a truck with a minister, and he thinks he's got to preach a sermon. Like the Salvation Army, except the food is shit. The preacher thinks he's got a special message for us, cause he's an Indian."

"So?" said Remo.

"No," said Lupin, "Cherokee. Funny eyes and everything. We let him hang around sometimes and trot him out for photographers."

The war council was being held in what was left of the pretty white church. Pretty on the outside. Inside, the pews were in disarray, the bibles torn, human feces stinking in corners. Men and women slept in pews. Some leaned, half-awake, against shattered stained-glass windows, trying to drain sips of whiskey from bottles that had run dry. The American flag was shredded over a shattered piano.

And there were guns. Handguns in belts, rifles cradled in arms, stacked against walls, piled up in corners. If someone had built an arsenal in a never cleaned lavatory, this would be it, thought Remo.

A man in braids and deerskin sat where the pulpit had been. He waved at Remo. "Keep that bastard outside. I don't know him."

"He knows how to get food," yelled Lupin. "And whiskey."

"Bring him here."

"That's Dennis Petty," said Lupin as he and Remo approached.

Petty looked down from the pulpit, a sneer rising from his thin lips. "He looks like another reporter," he said.

"He ain't, Petty," said Lupin.

Petty had a pale, almost shiny face that looked like a pocked victim of too many chocolate bars, milk shakes, and peanuts. He had a gold cap on a front tooth, which made his sneer look like an attempt to shine the tooth or at least to air it.

"How are you going to get us food and why?"

"I will lead a war party, a raiding party," said Remo.

"We had two hunting parties, and all we got for it were two dead cows, which are now rotting."

"That's because you don't know how to hunt," said Remo.

"I don't know how to hunt? I don't know how to hunt? I am supreme chief of the Sioux, of the Iroquis, of the Mohawk and Cheyenne and Dakota. Of the Arapaho and Navajo and . . ."

"Hey, boss, I think he can really get some food in here."

"Bullshit. He can't even stay alive," said Petty and snapped his fingers. "It is written that the supreme chief should not look upon blood while in council." Petty turned his back on the intruder, who obviously had not read the *New York Globe* or *Washington Post*. Otherwise, he would have recognized Petty immediately.

"I tried," said Remo's companion apologetically.

"Don't worry about it," said Remo. He saw five men approach him from the sacristy. One wore feathers, the others braids, like Petty. The feathered man slipped a switchblade out of his floppy poncho. He clicked open the blade.

"He's mine," he said.

The man made a low-line lunge, looking for a fast kill between Remo's ribs. Unfortunately for him, one does not make fast kills with knives when one's knife has lost contact with one's shoulder. And it is even more difficult when one's throat suddenly feels a thumb go through it and into one's spinal column.

Whistling "Nearer My God to Thee" in honor of what was left of the liberated church, Remo brought thumb and forefinger together and flipped the knife wielder into a back pew.

He caught the man with the longest braids and tied them tightly around the neck so that the war-paint on the face would have a nice blue back-ground. A simple step left and he took a forehead with a downcrack of the left hand. A step right and another crack on another forehead felled the fourth Indian revolutionary and left the fifth with a sudden vision. "You're my brother," he said to Remo. "Wel-come to the tribe."

Hearing this, Petty turned around and saw one man gurgling red from his throat, another choking to death on his own braids, and two others with ugly dark welts in their foreheads, lying against church pews, their most recent cares being their last forever.

"Welcome to the tribe," said Petty.

"Thank you, brother."

Suddenly the pew shook and the church shivered at its beams.

"What's that?" asked Remo.

"Nothing," said Dennis Petty. "We're blowing up the monument. Let's go see if the first blast did it."

"I'll bet the first one didn't," said Remo, breathing.

CHAPTER FOUR

There were worse posts than Vladivostok. At least it had electricity, and when you were assistant personnel officer for Russia's largest Pacific port, you could get a half-share of a television and your own one-room apartment.

Granted it was not a dacha outside Moscow and granted there were no limousines, but there was meat three times a week, and in the spring, there would be fresh melons imported from Korea, just across the Sea of Japan.

It could have been worse. In Stalin's era Valashnikov would be dead—with luck—or in one of those camps that stretched like a sea across Russia. Those who went to the camps were the living dead.

But this was a new Russia, that is, as new as Russia could ever be, and after the years of failing to find the Cassandra, he was spared a court martial for treason and allowed to employ his mind in the service of the People's Port of Vladivostok, where he watched a lot of Russian television. As he said to a friend, "A man truly is ready for the last sleep when he can watch Russian television hour after hour."

Valashnikov's dark eyes no longer shone with the precise brilliance of his younger years, and the flesh hung flabby from his jowls. The hair was gone except for graying tufts around his ears, and his fat belly protruded in front of him like a taut balloon. He wore an old silk bathrobe and sipped tea through a sugar cube he held between his teeth.

"Isn't Russian television the best television in the world?" asked his young friend, a pretty little girl of ten, with plump cheeks and almond eyes, who let him touch her all over if he gave her honeyed dates and coins.

"No. No. It's rather dull."

"You have seen other television?"

"Oh, yes. America. French. British."

"You've been to America?"

"I'm not allowed to say, my dear. Come. Sit by your old friend."

"With my panties on?"

"No. You know how I like them."

"Mamma says you should give me more money for this. But I'd rather have candy."

"Well, money is scarce. But I'll give you a lemon drop."

"I'd like to watch the news first. We must tell in school what we see on the news."

"I will tell you what the news will say. It will say capitalism is disintegrating, Communism is rising, but we must all be watchful for the fanatic revisionism of the Chinese warmongers abroad and for the secret fascist writers at home. There you have the official party view of the world. Now let me touch."

"If I can't watch," said the girl, "then I will have to tell my teacher why I didn't. What I was doing."

"Let us watch," said Valashnikov, outmaneuvered by a ten-year-old girl. If his great but now sleepy mind had not accumulated so much vast knowledge, he would have thought that this was the lowest point of his life. But he knew better. A man never sinks so low that he cannot sink even lower.

The news began with America disintegrating. Riots were sweeping the capitalist land. The Indians—the ragged remnants of the slaughtered tribes—were rising, trying to regain their stolen lands through a better knowledge of Marxist-Leninist theory, as taught by the true keepers of dialectic materialism and not by the Chinese revisionists.

"What is that?" asked the girl, pointing to the screen.

"That, my dear, is a monument to the massacre of a small band of American Indians in 1873, which their government at first kept secret and then acknowledged in the early 1960s, building a monument to their own perfidy. The monument is of black marble, is fifty feet long by twenty-five feet wide, and has a bronze plaque exactly twenty feet in diameter, set precisely in its center. It is a monument. Just a monument. Just a monument. Around it has grown the town of Wounded Elk, whose inhabitants are the Apowa. Those men in imitation Indian clothes are not Apowa. I know about Apowa. What you are seeing is not Apowa, but don't tell anyone. No

Apowa, I might add, has ever worked for the United States government in any official capacity, nor has one ever taken a course in nuclear physics. An estimated hundred thousand people now visit Wounded Elk each year, this being attributed to a book by one Lynn Cosgrove.

"Miss Cosgrove never worked for the United States government, either, being originally a member of the Socialist Party. Nor was she paid by the CIA to write the book.

"There are no military installations within forty miles of the monument, and the only government employee there is one man who visits the monument once a month to mow the grass and wash the marble.

"Would you like to know that man's name, age, education, and speech habits? Would you like to know the name of the motel that man lives in? You should. Your labor paid for it. So did my career, as a matter of fact.

"The man who cleans the monument is beyond a shadow of a doubt, a cleaning man. The Union of Soviet Socialist Republics spent two full weeks finding out that the cleaning man was truly a cleaning man. From womb to washpan, that man is a cleaning man.

"And do you know why it was so important? Because we had to make sure that monument was a monument. If it weren't a monument, it would need a technician or a scientist, not a cleaning man, once a month. A Geiger counter, not a broom. But the cleaning man was colored."

"What color?" asked the girl as the television

screen showed people parading around the prairie near the monument. It was a stupid question.

"Lavender," said Valashnikov sarcastically.

"There are many colors a person can be," said the girl, pushing herself away from the fat old man.

"I'm sorry, my dear," said Valashnikov. "He was tan—Negro, African, black. There are no black nuclear physicists operating in America. Therefore—and this was the final proof—the man was a cleaning man. Many blacks in America are cleaning men, because of racism, my dear, which comes from capitalism and which we, the true Marxist-Leninist state, are free of. Now get your plump little ass over here or get the hell out of my apartment.

"White people turn brown in the summer," said the girl defensively. "We learned that in school. The capitalist oppressors go south during the winter to turn brown, and then they return north to keep the real brown people out of their palaces and castles, built with the sweat and blood of the laboring class."

"A top agent," shouted Valashnikov, "would not confuse a summer tan with a race!" The girl clutched her panties, which were half-off, snapped them up over her behind, and grabbing her books, ran from the apartment. Just then Valashnikov spotted on his television a kimono with a pattern he immediately recognized as Korean—Vladivostok was just a short trip away from the friendly northern part of that country. He saw the kimono get into a car, where a familiar looking man in a light suit sat behind the wheel. Valashnikov had seen the face before, in color photographs taken near the end of his career. But now the face on black and white television appeared white. And the features, which he had always thought had a high degree of Caucasian about them, now on the screen looked absolutely Caucasian. Valashnikov slapped his forehead with his open palm.

"Of course. Of course."

Now the announcer was launching his heavy explanation of what was happening in the capitalist state. But Valashnikov was not listening. He was shouting joyfully at the television, "Not cleaning man! Not cleaning man! Not cleaning man!"

Laughing aloud, Valashnikov dressed quickly and ran out of the door, past the candy dish. Since he had come to Vladivostok, he had not once left his apartment without taking a piece of candy. But now there was no time for it. He ran, chugging, laughing, perspiring in the muggy port heat, to his office, which had a telephone.

He dialed Moscow. Since the number of KGB's foreign branch changed every few months, he had long since lost access to it, and now he was talking to KGB local, which could cover anything from counterintelligence to selling tomatoes on the black market.

"This is Colonel Ivan Ivanovich Valashnikov, and if you don't recognize my name, your superiors will remember it. I must get to Moscow immediately . . . No. I am not currently colonel. I am colonel retired. I must get to Moscow immediately . . . No, I cannot tell you . . . Then, damn you, get me a military priority on aircraft leaving Vladivostok . . . Yes, yes, I know . . . I am Ivan Ivanovich Valashnikov, and I am assistant personnel officer, and yes, I know what I risk by demanding immediate flight. Yes, I understand that I may fly in one of your special aircraft but that if this is a game or drunken trick, I will take a train out to one of the camps. Yes, I agree. You may phone me back."

And Valashnikov hung up and waited. Ten minutes later the office phone rang. It was a higher ranking KGB officer. His voice was kindly. Didn't Valashnikov want to think it over before he claimed such importance for his mission? The officer had Valashnikov's record in front of him and he saw what appeared to be a career of major importance that had come to a standstill over an obsession with something that was marked Top Secret in the file. That kind of top secret, out of reach of the KGB officer, was an area that showed failure bordering on treason.

Now, didn't Comrade Valashnikov want to think over his urgent request for an aircraft to Moscow? Perhaps he could write down his findings and give them to Vladivostok KGB so an officer could examine them and forward them to the proper office. If Comrade Valashnikov were wrong, then no harm would be done to him or anyone else.

"But I say it is a crisis," Valashnikov said, "and now you may refuse to order me a plane. I will preface my written report by stating that I spoke to you at four fifteen P.M. and requested immediate transportation for a maximum-security matter of crisis proportions but you advised me to put it all in a letter."

Valashnikov heard the gulp that traveled thousands

of miles across Siberia from the capital. He had the officer in a box. It was wonderful to feel the power again, to be able to move men just through the power and ability of one's mind.

"Sir, is that your position?"

"That is my position," said Valashnikov, tears welling up in his eyes with the joy of his returning manhood. "We have an international advantage, and I am warning you, every moment might mean its loss."

"Wait at your office. Because of your former position, I am going to authorize private and immediate treatment for transportation for you, Valashnikov, but let me warn you . . ."

"You're wasting time, son," said Valashnikov and hung up. He realized he was trembling and wanted a drink or a sedative. No. He would not have one.

The tension was delicious. But maybe he was wrong. He had seen the picture only briefly. Maybe because the girl had talked about tans and races and that was on his mind, he had only imagined that picture was of the man who visited the monument once a month to mow and trim. Maybe he had been away from the halls of power too long? What if he was wrong? He could be wrong. It was only a fleeting glimpse of the white-haired man in the car.

And then his great mind began to work, isolating and reducing all the facts to a very simple one: What if he was wrong? Was death any worse really than his life? Hadn't he made calculations for possible magadeaths in nuclear wars when he was in Moscow? Now he was making another calculation. This time for a single death. It was worth it. He would proceed, no matter what, on the assumption that the marble and bronze monument ont the Montana prairie was the Cassandra.

No matter what fact came up, he would assume it was a camouflage. If he were to be shown the top of the monument being removed and if he were to stand on bare earth and then watch the earth being removed by shovels, he would still function on the premise that the Cassandra was there. He had committed his life to it. What else did he have to lose? Nothing.

He heard a knock at his office door, and before he could say, "Come in," the door opened.

Two men in KGB street uniforms of blazing colors, with gold epaulets and shining boots, marched into the office. They were followed by a plainclothesman, a man Valashnikov had always thought of as the superintendent of his building, a man of no major importance.

The man carried a cardboard valise that Valashnikov recognized as his own, even to the tears on the leather straps around it. The man snapped his fingers and another KGB officer led in the girl who had fled his apartment.

"Yes," said Valashnikov.

"Are you ready for your flight?" asked the man Valashnikov had thought of as his building superintendent.

"Yes," said Valashnikov coolly. "What is the girl doing here?"

"For your pleasure, comrade. Your file shows you are pleased with her."

"Get her out of here," said Valashnikov. His voice carried the hard precision of authority.

Hearing this, the girl cried.

Valashnikov emptied his pocket of bills and knelt down, pressing them into her hands.

"Little girl, just a few hours ago I thought that there was no bottom to life. Now I see it also has no top. Do not cry. Here is money for your mother. You are nice little girl. Go home."

"You don't want me," sobbed the girl.

"As a granddaughter I would want you, my dear, but no other way. You grow up and stay away from old men. All right? All right?"

The girl sniffled and nodded. Valashnikov gave her a tender kiss on the cheek and took his bag from the superintendent, who smiled weakly and shrugged.

"You will take her home, Comrade Superintendent. Without touching. I will check on you from Moscow."

And Valashnikov felt good because he had recognized the face of a white man, a man who could only be taken for a black as a result of bureaucratic error.

Tan, not Negro, thought Valashnikov as he left his office for a plane that would take him back to Moscow. And perhaps back to his career.

CHAPTER FIVE

Remo saw the two men in blue jeans and flannel shirts stringing wire from the monument, and he suggested to them that they stop what they were doing.

Obviously, this rather thin stranger impressed them because they immediately dropped their wire spools and fell to the Montana dust, clutching their groins.

"Thanks, fellas," said Remo.

"What did you do that for?" asked Petty shrilly.

"I got a better idea," said Remo.

"How can you have a better idea? *Newstime* says my command structure is immaculate. The networks called this takeover 'smooth.' The wire services have quoted federal marshals as saying I am incredibly well organized. You can't go hitting my men without my orders."

"I'm sorry, but blowing up that dinky monument," said Remo, pointing to the massive marble base, "is a one-shot deal. Then all you have is a hole in the ground. That's all you're occupying. So long, television coverage."

A group of the revolutionaries from the church who

were still able to stand began forming around them. From the back of the crowd, Burning Star, nee Lynn Cosgrove, let out a low, moaning wail.

"What is that?" asked Petty.

"It's an Indian chant," said a man standing near him.

"How the hell would you know?" asked Petty.

"I saw it in *Blazing Arrows*, starring Randolph Scott and Victor Mature. And besides, I'm your minister of cultural affairs." He punctuated his sentence by draining the last of his pint bottle of Old Grand Dad and angrily flinging the bottle against the marble monument, where it hit a tarpaulin and bounced to the ground without breaking.

"Brothers, brothers!" cried Burning Star. "Do not listen to the forked tongue of the white man. We must destroy that monument to oppression or we can never be men again. What is our manhood under the rule of the white man but drinking, gambling, and robbing? Our heritage calls for wiping out the vestiges of white oppression."

"Yeah, yeah, yeah!" shouted several gunbearers. Remo heard several war whoops.

"Brothers!" cried Remo. "If we destroy the monument, we have nothing. But if you come with me on a raiding party, we will have steaks and chops and cakes and beer and french fries and ice cream and all good things."

"Who are you?" demanded the minister of cultural affairs.

"And whiskey," yelled Remo.

In the spirit of the great raid, the minister of

cultural affairs punched Burning Star in the face.

"To the great raid," yelled Chief Petty.

"To the great raid," yelled the ambulatory members of the Revolutionary Indian Party.

"What about our heritage?" cried someone else. Seeing that it was a woman, Jerry Lupin let her have it right between her braids with his rifle butt. Her boyfriend circled the crowd after Lupin, who found a spot close to Remo, then gave the boyfriend a central finger waving in the blue Montana sky.

The boyfriend made a fist, silently threatening to take the matter up later. Lupin pressed two fingers together to signal that he and Remo were close.

Petty waved everyone to silence. "We will raid. I appoint this man my raid chief, chief of raid."

There were whoops of approval.

"Watch out for the Apowa when you get out of here," whispered Petty to Remo. "They hate us. Hate us with a passion. If it wasn't for the feds ringing this place, we might all be dead. Those Apowas can be mean. You sure you can get a raiding party in and out, past the marshals?"

"Guaranteed," said Remo.

"With trucks?"

"How many people you got here?"

"About forty. And if you're getting ice cream, caramel fudge for me—and not the diet junk. You know, real ice cream."

Remo winked his assurances, and Petty put an arm around his shoulder.

"But the monument is mine," said Remo. "You

leave it to me. I got something really great for the monument."

"What?" asked Petty anxiously.

"Half hour prime time," said Remo. "But you can't blow up the monument."

"We never had prime time before," said Petty. "The six o'clock news, the evening news, and of course that columnist from the *New York Globe* who writes my press releases and takes orders from us. He's the one who did the public relations for the Attica prison riot. But he's nowhere near prime time."

"Half hour," said Remo.

Remo followed the wires to the large, flat monument. From ground level it looked like a gigantic fallen tombstone. He hopped up onto the marble base and saw where the previous dynamite blast had chipped away pieces of the bronze. He felt his stomach weaken and his mouth go very dry.

He knew that what was beneath his feet could turn this prairie, this state, and many surrounding states to deep holes in the ground. And somehow, even though his mind told him that death was death, whether by hurled stone or other guided missile, there was something more terrifying about being in the center of a nuclear holocaust.

Following death, the body normally rots and is broken down into other substances. And while Remo believed that death ended it all, somehow it was still part of continuing life, even if you were just fertilizer for a daisy. But a nuclear holocaust destroys matter. It doesn't just burn it into gases that float away or leave a carbon cinder—it simply eliminates matter from existence. And there was enough nuclear power under Remo's feet to eliminate most of the matter from the Rockies on the west to the Appalachians on the east.

Remo bent down and unsnapped the two strands leading to the sticks of dynamite. Holding them in his hand, he felt safer. Then he went to every one of RIP's forty-man army of occupation and made sure they had no more dynamite. He found one of the explosives men in the bathroom of the church.

"You ain't telling me what to do, buddy," said the man, still angry about being kicked in the groin. If I want to blow that frigging hunk of rock, I'm gonna blow that frigging hunk of rock."

Remo reasoned with him. He explained that to the man that, perhaps, he was being a bit childish. Perhaps this hostile immaturity stemmed from a lack of proper toilet training. Remo understood. He understood the basic problems deriving from earliest childhood. And he knew that what the man really needed was not to blow up a monument. No, the man needed proper toilet training.

"Oh, yeah," said the man, smirking at the kinky runt who had gotten in a lucky punch before out at the monument when all he'd been doing was stringing the wires for the blast.

"Yeah," repeated Remo as he reintroduced the man to the toilet in exact reverse of the way his parents had done it more than two decades before. This time there were no complaints, no requests to leave potty, none of the psychological damage that comes from too early an introduction to modern man's bowel control. There were just a few bubbles in the bowl, and then there was nothing. The man slumped, chin over toilet lip, water dripping from his mouth, his eyes blank. Remo rammed the dynamite sticks down the dead throat into the cooling intestines where they would be safe.

Twenty braves had gathered in the growing dusk outside the church, volunteers for the great raid. Lynn Cosgrove wanted to come along.

"But keep your mouth shut," said Remo. "And you, Lupin, stop hitting her in the face."

"I was only trying to help," said Lupin.

"Leave her alone," Remo said.

"I will chronicle your brave exploits," said Burning Star. "How the brave bands raised their pure hearts to the buffalo and to the elk, how the braves set out to make America beautiful again, a home where clear waters run from mother ocean and high big mountain."

Remo gently placed a finger over Burning Star's swollen lips. "We're going to rip off a liquor store and a supermarket, not storm the Bastille," he said.

"The liquor store and the supermarket are our Bastille," said Burning Star.

"We are all Bastilles," yelled someone raising a Kalashnikov.

"Shut up or you don't eat," said Remo.

There was silence on the Montana prairie except for the buzzing noise from the far-off circle of newsmen. Remo could see their lights and trailers and tents. In the darkness, atop a hill to the left, was the town of Wounded Elk, populated by Apowas who

73

would, if Petty were acurate, kill anyone from RIP. And in the center of this mess was the end of America under a loose bronze plate that had almost gone with the first blast.

Far beyond the circle of newsmen and marshals was the motel where Chiun was watching Van Riker, who was supposed to be calculating something scientific that Remo hoped he would keep to himself.

At least no one would be blowing off the nuclear cap with dynamite, thought Remo, as he told his band to keep quiet and follow him.

"And lo, onto the dark trail went the mighty band, first among them the man called Remo, and then upon that trail, the Oglala and the Chippewa, the Nez Percé and the Navaho, the Mohawk and the Cheyenne, the . . ."

"Shut up, Cosgrove, or you're not coming," said Remo.

As they went clanging noisily through the trench in front of the monument, Remo realized they weren't going to make it. Too much noise. So as they moved toward the line of federal marshals, Remo tapped one and then another, telling each to go back. As they approached the first federal outpost, Remo was left with one, but he knew that one quiet moving person was better than a crowd. He did not even notice who the person was, but he knew good balanced movements when he heard them, that internal sort of walk that kept energy centralized.

"Put your hand on my back and follow me," said Remo. "Wherever I move, you move, and move slowly, nothing fast."

Feeling the hand on his back, Remo walked stealthily over the soft earth. When there was silence, he stopped. When there was buzzing, he moved forward, each movement attuned to the earth and the people. Spotting a slouching, bored marshal who seemed to have turned off his senses, he crept to within fifteen feet of the man. Then he stepped out into the light, grabbed the person behind him, and spun around so he and his companion appeared to be running toward the monument instead of away from it.

"Follow me," said Remo loudly. "We got by him."

"You there, halt!" shouted the marshal. "Come back here."

"Bastard," said Remo glumly.

"You people could have gotten yourselves killed trying to get past me," said the marshal. He tilted back his blue baseball cap with the federal emblem on it. "Don't try it again."

"Okay, you win," said Remo, his hands in the air. He and his companion walked past the guard toward a crowd of newsmen.

"And lo, the brave warrior named Remo, who walked in darkness, moved with pure heart . . ."

"Shut up, Cosgrove," said Remo, realizing it was Burning Star who had the best balance of the band he had started with.

"She's in deerskin," said the marshal. "Is she a newsman or what?"

"She's a newsman," said Remo.

"A newsperson," said Burning Star.

"Shut up, Cosgrove," said Remo.

"Call me Burning Star."

"Where did you learn to move like that? That's better than a karate black belt," Remo said.

"Ballet," said Burning Star.

"Hah. So much for tribal heritage," said Remo.

"You look Indian," said Burning Star. "I realized it back there. You are Indian, aren't you?"

"I wouldn't know," said Remo honestly. "In my recent training, I've learned that the world is made up of Koreans and a bunch of other people."

Seeing Burning Star in deerskin, several newsmen attempted to interview her, but Remo quietly explained to her that they had to lose the newsmen because it was not the wisest thing to steal a truck on coast-to-coast television.

Telling the most persistent newsman that yes, she believed the Euro dollar would come back into its own if the gold market steadied, she ducked behind a network truck. Remo explained to the driver that he had to move the truck because he didn't have residual clearance.

"Wha?" asked the driver leaning out of the cab. Remo explained the rest carefully, leaving him somewhat unconscious underneath a nearby car.

"Couldn't you get anything less conspicuous than a network broadcasting truck?" asked Burning Star with a toss of her long, straight red hair.

"Around here?" asked Remo. As they drove out of the improvised parking lot, Remo suddenly noticed how fine Burning Star's features were, how the night

76

light played on her soft cheeks, and how her breasts swelled under the deerskin.

"You know," said Burning Star. "You're an attractive man. Very attractive."

"I was thinking something along those lines myself," said Remo. But then he felt the truck shudder, and he stopped thinking about such things, even though he realized as they sped down the highway that the bump was just a soft shoulder of the road. He parked in front of the motel where Chiun and Van Riker were.

He left Burning Star in the truck and went in to find Chiun watching the last of the taped shows. Ever since the networks had stretched soap operas to ninety minutes and two hours, he had been watching the delayed shows later and later.

It was nine thirty P.M.

Remo sat on the motel bed, waiting patiently as one sister refused to go to another sister's welcome-home party because she was jealous of the sister's success and the mother wanted to know why, especially since the famous sister was really dying of cancer and had difficulty speaking to boys.

Remo made sure that even the last commercial was over before he spoke.

"Where's Van Riker?"

"Where he will not ruin the rhythms of art," said Chiun.

"What did you do with him? You're supposed to keep him alive. You didn't kill him, did you? We're supposed to keep him alive. Alive means breathing,

77

even if breathing should interfere for one moment with your pleasure."

"I am well aware of the instructions from Emperor Smith and how you slavishly follow them. I am aware that some men achieve Sinanju and others are mired in the slavishness of servants, no matter how perfect the training or the master who administers it. Smith, being white, would not know the difference between an assassin and a servant."

"Where's Van Riker?"

"Where he cannot harm the simple pleasure of a gentle sweet soul taking meager comfort in the golden years of his mellow life."

Remo heard snoring.

"You locked him in the bathroom, didn't you?"

"I didn't have a dungeon," said Chiun by way of explanation.

Remo snapped open the door without bothering to unlock it. Van Riker, who had been sleeping against the door, tumbled out, his plans on his chest.

"Oh," he said. He got to his feet, straightened himself out, organized his papers, and noted that he had never been treated so disrespectfully.

"Neither has the master of Sinanju," said Chiun. "Remo, how much longer must I endure this torrent of abuse, this incessant squawking?"

"All I said was . . ."

"Shhh," said Remo, putting a finger to his lips. "Listen, I don't have much time. They tried to blast off the bronze cap with dynamite."

"Oh, my God," said Van Riker.

"Sit down, sit down. There's some good news. I can guarantee no one there knows that it's the Cassandra."

"I told you. They tried to blast off the cap. Would they do that if they knew?"

"That's right. I was just so shocked. Will they try again?"

"I doubt it. I hid the dynamite."

"Good. So far. I've got to get in there to check on certain radiation leakages." To explain himself, Van Riker drew diagrams of what he called critical mass and various other things that made only vague sense to Remo.

"Look, let me put it this way," said Van Riker. "I've got to measure the damned thing to see if it's going to go off. I can do it. I know how to do it. I do it every month. There isn't one nuclear device in there—there are five and . . ."

"All right, all right, all right," Remo said. "We'll get you into Wounded Elk tonight."

Van Riker went to the closet, where he got the special broom he had shown the Oriental before.

"What's that?" asked Remo.

"It's a geiger counter," said Van Riker. "It was my little extra touch to the whole Cassandra plan. One of the details that made it work."

"It worked so well," said Chiun, "we are all here waiting to be ashes."

"It worked so well," said Van Riker, the blood rushing to his tanned neck, "that the Russians have been kept at bay for more than a decade. And possibly,

79

sir, in some small part because a gieger counter looked like a broom."

Across the globe, in a room without windows in a complex called the Kremlin in a city called Moscow, someone else was making the same point.

And the top brass was listening as they had not listened since the speaker was a young man who could explain scientific ramifications to military men and military ramifications to scientific men and international politics to all of them.

CHAPTER SIX

There was some unexpected trouble from the diplomatic liaison. Valashnikov did not sit down, nor did he leave the map of the United States, nor did he—as his most recent instincts would command—move apologetically to a side seat among the many generals and field marshals waiting for the diplomatic liaison to make his point.

Smiling, Valashnikov leaned his right knuckles on the edge of the table, almost touching the chairman of the Russian People's Defense Forces. "Are you through?" he asked the diplomatic liaison. "Or do you want intelligence to ask Military Intelligence?"

"There are some questions we have," the official answered, questions we feel perhaps should have been asked by Military Intelligence before we were called here at the drop of a hat to hear an assistant personnel officer for a Pacific port tell us about military imbalances that might become political imbalances that would give us the entire world—which we could not occupy on such short notice, anyway."

"One does not have to occupy a land with troops

to control it. Go ahead, comrade," said Valashnikov crisply.

"Does it not seem strange, comrade, that this gigantic, dirty bomb—for that is what Cassandra is, a gigantic, dirty bomb at the end of a missile—does it not seem strange to you that the Americans would leave it lying out in the middle of a prairie? A prairie, by the way, that is the site of an injustice perpetrated against a minority in revolution? Eh? Strange? Eh?"

"Yes," said Valashnikov with the calm of a frozen lake, and the generals exchanged little glances indicating that a man had just very quickly ended a career and possibly a life by surrendering this major point.

"Yes," Valashnikov repeated. "It is totally absurd. Or would be if Cassandra had been built today and not in the early 1960s. In the early 1960s there was a different American Indian. There was a different everything in America. At that time the safest place for anything was an Indian reservation, which, I might add, comrade, tended to keep whites out. And yellows out."

"But there was a road right to the monument?"

"Right. And it was not even paved until a book made the site famous," said Valashnikov. "Until the road was paved, it was just good enough for military trucks to bring in missile components."

Diplomatic Liaison shook his head. "It is not that I am trying desperately to protect the détente. Détente with America is just another step in our foreign policy. It doesn't mean a change in anything. It is a tool to be discarded when no longer useful. What I am afraid of is reckless endangerment of this tool of détente because *you* saw a picture on a television screen."

"And had it made into a still, in which I have positively identified a nuclear engineer by the name of Douglas Van Riker, lieutenant general, United States Air Force—"

"Whom you have for years assumed was a cleaning man who went to the monument every month, a cleaning man who was positively identified by our own KGB as a cleaning man."

Valashnikov clapped his hands loudly and beamed. "Which, comrade, has thrown me off for years. For years. I had assumed that the monument could not be the Cassandra. And why? Because of a report by the KGB. Now this is not a criticism. The KGB was right . . . in overall policy. I had devoted a career to finding that missile-bomb, and I had failed. After seeing failure after failure on my part, the KGB was most correct in moving its better agents to more crucial areas."

Valashnikov caught a nod from the KGB liaison. It meant that having been vindicated, his organization would allow itself to admit a minor slip, especially if it were part of an overall correct attitude.

"So," said Valashnikov, "a less competent agent was assigned. An agent who listed the cleaning man as tan. Now when the report came back, also to a minor department, *tan* was read as *brown*, which was translated to *Negro*, which was translated right back to *cleaning man*. At that time there were no Negro nuclear physicists or nuclear engineers. But let us, comrades, translate *tan* back to *tan*, and we will find that there is a nuclear engineer who lives in the Bahamas and has a very nice tan. His name is Van Riker, our own General Van Riker, who was seen at Wounded Elk, albeit partially blocked out by the kimono of someone in his car." Valashnikov looked around the table.

"I congratulate you," said Diplomatic Liaison. "But for one thing, you have made a good case. If that monument were the Cassandra, would the American government not move in to protect it against the demonstrators, lest the very center of the country blow up? If we had a Cassandra, it would be protected by division upon division upon division. Now would you have us believe a ring of United States marshals are sitting placidly by while a bunch of renegades dance over their special doomsday device? Be realistic. Be realistic, comrade."

"You forget, comrade," said Valashnikov, "that Cassandra's best defense has always been the fact that we did not know where it is."

"And we did not know where it is," said Diplomatic Liaison, "because it never existed. Yes, it is my conclusion that it never existed. I too am aware of how strong America was vis-à-vis Russia in the early 1960s. Wouldn't it have been clever of them to waste our resources looking for a nonexistent bomb?"

"Cassandra," said Valashnikov, "was the name of a prophetess of doom in Western literature. No one listened to her. She had the power to see the future, but her curse was that no one would listen. Perhaps the American vehicle of death was aptly named, after all. Perhaps just for a moment such as this, so we would listen before making a miscalculation."

There was quiet in the room. Then Diplomatic Liaison spoke. "You have not addressed yourself to the question of why there is no protection of Cassandra right now. No country would leave something that dangerous unprotected. At the mercies of a band of lunatics."

Valashnikov saw the KGB liaison nod assent. The admiral of the fleet nodded assent. The general of the missile forces nodded assent. All the important heads were nodding, and Valashnikov was lost. Then the chief of KGB snapped his fingers twice.

"Flash that photograph of Van Riker again," he said. An assistant immediately darkened a screen area and put in the proper slide.

"That design on the kimono at the car door . . . I've seen it before. Recently, in the last year," said KGB. "Where have I seen it?"

"It is a Korean rendering of a Chinese ideograph, sir," said an aide.

"But what? Where have I seen it? It came across my desk, and if it came across my desk, it had to be important."

"The ideograph means 'absolute' or 'master,'" said the aide. "The letter had something to do with Sinanju, an employment query. Assassins, sir, a rather ancient house of them."

"And what was the disposition of that request to work for us?"

"There wasn't exactly any disposition, sir. It was a long, rambling letter about the lack of appreciation

85

in a young country for assassins and how the House of Sinanju was looking for a new employer once it could successfully retrieve its investment from the pale ingrates."

"Investment? What investment?" asked the chief of the KGB.

"Well, sir, we couldn't quite make it out." He paused. The letter seemed not really the sort of thing one brought before the military leaders of a nation. It was better suited for a weepy romance novel. "Sir, the investment was in the training of a white man, to whom the master gave the best years of his life. It goes on at length, sir, about various forms of ingratitude. It seems, sir, highly self-pitying."

"So how does a crackpot letter wind up on my desk?"

"Sir, Sinanju is not what we classify as crackpot. The house of assassins once worked for the Romanovs, and the letter specifically referred to Ivan the Great. We found references to Sinanju in the czar's archives. It seems he was fond of them and they of him. In any case, sir, when the revolution came, we dispensed with what had been a yearly retainer."

"Why?"

"Idealism. This house has been associated with every reactionary regime since the Ming Dynasty."

"Would you call this Sinanju thing effective protection? I mean, one man?"

"That's just why it was on your desk, sir. Yes, sir. In some cases, far superior to a division. Sinanju was the original creator of hand fighting. It is called the sun source of the martial arts."

"That man in the kimono looks old."

"According to the archives, the master of Sinanju who served Czar Ivan was ninety when he slaughtered a Cossack troop for the entertainment of the czar."

There was a hushed clearing of throats in the room. Then Diplomatic Liaison spoke: "Well, Valashnikov, congratulations on finding your Cassandra. You must confirm it, of course."

"Yes," said KGB. "You are also authorized to hire that Sinanju person. We are at your full disposal."

"You know, if we can definitely pinpoint the Cassandra—without any doubt—there are limitless nuclear variations we can employ," said the commander of Russian missile forces. And in that room they knew what no one else knew at the time: that the balance of nuclear power in the world might just have been unalterably changed because an aide recognized a Korean symbol.

But what they did not know was that while the master of Sinanju liked their police state tactics and thought very highly of their very quick judicial system, to him there was not much difference between the tanned, white-haired nuisance with the Geiger counter and the others who called themselves Communists. They were all white to him. He even had some difficulty in telling them apart.

CHAPTER SEVEN

"How many must we be forced to kill in the liberation of our land?" asked Burning Star as she and Remo sped through the night toward the Apowa village of Wounded Elk. "How many must die in our search for the buffalo before the great eagle nests in the cliffs of his father's home?"

"You mean at the Apowa supermarket?" asked Remo. Up ahead he saw the cluster of lights, a flashing neon arrow, and a huge neon sign that read, "Big A Plaza—Open Late."

"At the new buffalo hunting grounds, yes. Will we slay tens or hundreds or tens of hundreds to liberate our sacred buffalo and return his skin to the lodge where men can look upon themselves as men and not as helpless children driven by the white man's alcohol to debase themselves and their sacred heritage."

"We're going to pay for the food it that's what you're asking."

"But it is our food. Our buffalo. While I condemn the killing itself, I can understand why we must do this. To bring attention to the injustices done our people."

"I've got a pocketful of money," said Remo. "And I'd just as soon pay for the goods. Besides, do you want to load the truck?"

Burning Star shook her head, her bright red curls flashing from side to side. "As our ancestors were robbed of their land, so shall we rob these oppressors of their stolen buffalo."

"Hey, Cosgrove," said Remo, pulling into the lot, "these stores are all owned by full-blooded Apowas."

"They are Sacajaweas."

"Sacks of what?"

"Sacajawea. She was the traitor who guided Lewis and Clark across our land."

"So that makes it all right for someone named Cosgrove to steal from Apowas?"

"If we burn babies, have they not burned our babies? If we burn them alive in their white-man's houses, have they not burned us in our tents? We are standing against oppression and . . ."

As they drove into the Big A parking lot, Lynn Cosgrove was suddenly silent. She had not seen Remo's hand move, but she felt a sudden stinging in her throat and realized that no words would come out.

Remo found the manager of the store and negotiated a purchase of frozen foods and instant dinners.

"I don't think there's anyone at the church who could baste a turkey," said Remo to the manager, who, like all supermarket managers, was harried to the point of exhaustion at the end of the day and managed with great effort to cover it all with a bright smile. But when Remo said "the church," the smile vanished from the reddish tan face and the dark eyes set in the high Indian cheekbones no longer welcomed Remo.

"This is for the thugs who took over our church?"

"They gotta eat, too."

"Have you been there?"

"Well, yes," said Remo.

"Did they really spread excrement on our church?"

"Well, they'll be pushed out soon."

"You're damned right, they're going to be pushed out soon," said the store manager, tears welling up in his dark eyes.

"What do you mean by that?" asked Remo.

"None of your business. You wanted food. You got food."

"I want to know what you meant by that. I mean, people could get hurt. Killed. A lot of people."

"Then a lot of people will get killed."

"The federal marshals will move them out," Remo said.

"No doubt, some day. A .155 millimeter howitzer will move 'em out a lot faster, I'll tell you that. Without any real Indians having to get killed, either. And without even having to say howdy to a fed."

Remo thought of a .155 millimeter cannon shell smashing into the monument. He thought of the Cassandra going up. All five nuclear devices going up. Montana going up. Large sections of Canada going up without anyone missing them. Wyoming and Colorado and Michigan and Kansas and Illinois

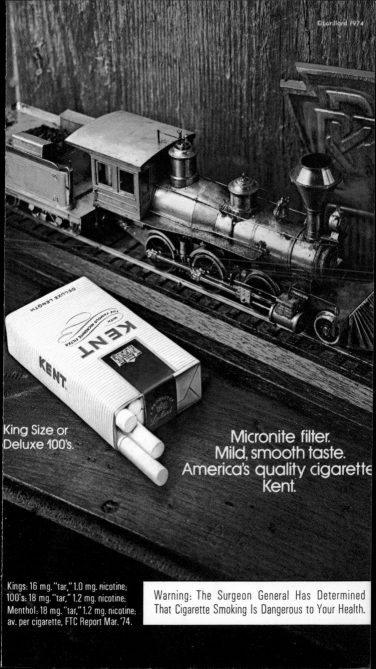

©Lorillard 1974

KENT

King Size or
Deluxe 100's.

Micronite filter.
Mild, smooth taste.
America's quality cigarette
Kent.

Kings: 16 mg. "tar," 1.0 mg. nicotine;
100's: 18 mg. "tar," 1.2 mg. nicotine;
Menthol: 18 mg. "tar," 1.2 mg. nicotine;
av. per cigarette, FTC Report Mar. '74.

Try the crisp, clean taste of Kent Menthol.

The only Menthol with the famous Micronite filter.

Kings: 16 mg. "tar," 1.0 mg. nicotine;
00's: 18 mg. "tar," 1.2 mg. nicotine;
Menthol: 18 mg. "tar," 1.2 mg. nicotine;
av. per cigarette, FTC Report Mar. '74.

Warning: The Surgeon General Has Determined
That Cigarette Smoking Is Dangerous to Your Health.

and Indiana and Ohio and all points east and west—one big nuclear flame.

"You got a great idea there, buddy," Remo said, "but you don't want to go firing away willy-nilly at your own church."

"We can rebuild it. We built it with our own hands the first time to commemorate what the monument now commemorates. We thought that if the government could build a monument there, we could build one, too. The church is our monument. You know, if the *New York Globe* columnist didn't insist on talking to those thieves and crooks from Chicago, he'd find out what a real Indian feels. Not some schoolroom, alley-ghetto philosophy."

"You won't have to rebuild the church. How would you like to get a clean shot at Dennis Petty? With your bare hands?"

When Remo said "bare hands," he saw a joyous lust in the store manager's eyes.

"Will you have that daffy bitch who started this nonsense with that book? Will you have her for us? That burning planet?"

"Burning Star? Cosgrove. Lynn Cosgrove?"

"Yes," said the store manager.

"If you don't blow up your own church."

"You've got an hour. Make it an hour and a half," said the store manager. "Could you make it five minutes?"

"Wait. I need time," Remo said.

"It ain't your church they're shitting in," said the store manager. "What the hell do you whites know

91

about what's sacred and what isn't? You come into our lands and desecrate them. You leave us the scrapings, and when we make out on those, you come into the places we built and crap all over them."

"Not me," said Remo. "The Revolutionary Indian Party."

"Yeah. Indian. Hah! This is Apowa country. Would a Frenchman let a German come in and tear down Notre Dame just because the German's white, too? Why the hell should we Apowa put up with this crap from those fucking half-breeds who want ot paint their faces and go shooting up our cows?"

"No reason," said Remo. "I'll have them for you in a day. Now where's the Howitzer?"

"None of your business, white man. But I promise you this. I'll be reasonable. You get me those bums, those desecrators, and I'll give you one day. Sunrise, day after tomorrow. More than a day because this is an Indian's gift to you."

"The day after tomorrow. Right. Who should I look for? I mean I can't just ask for the Indian giver."

"Do you want my real name or the legal one?"

"Whatever people know you by."

"My legal name is Wayne Ramage Henderson Hubbard Mason Woodleaf Kelley Brandt."

"Let's try your real name."

"Promise you won't laugh?"

"I got through your legal name with a straight face, didn't I?"

"It's He Who Walks like Cougar at Night."

92

"You got a serial number people know you by?" asked Remo.

"What's your name, big shot?" asked Brandt defensively.

"Remo."

He Who Walks like Cougar at Night called people over to hear the funny name, and after they all had a good laugh, they loaded the network truck with frozen dinners and shrimp bottled in their own cocktail sauce and Captain Crunch sugar-coated cereal, and seven cases of Twinkies.

"Good. Our buffalo," said Burning Star when she regained her voice and saw the goods being loaded on the network truck. Remo hit her again where he'd hit her before, and Burning Star was quiet.

He drove to the marshal's lines outside the Wounded Elk church, but then could not find his stolen marshal's badge.

He flashed a piece of cellophane at one of the marshals. "United States Federal Justice Department," he said with authority.

"That's a damned Twinkie wrapper," said the young federal marshal with the dark blue baseball cap and carbine. The cap had the American eagle on it.

"Not every plan is flawless," said Remo, and he snatched the carbine by its barrel, gave the kid a healthy zonk on the side of the head, and drove on toward the monument and church. Just in time, because Lynn Cosgrove's voice was returning and she was beginning the chant of the brave hunter returning with buffalo for the tribe.

The master of Sinanju made his way into Wounded Elk in a different manner. When the night was at its darkest, he donned his black night kimono and signaled Van Riker that they must go.

The peculiar white man wore a suit that reflected light, one of the chemical fabrics so common in the West. He carried that funny broom which was supposed to tell if the potential disaster he had created was going to come true. How strange, these Westerners, creating weapons that are bigger dangers to themselves than to their enemies, thought Chiun. But he remained quiet because if fools wished to destroy themselves, even he and all his ancestors could not protect them from themselves.

"You must change that suit," said Chiun.

"No can do, Papasan," said General Van Riker. "This suit protects me against radioactivity."

"How can a dead man be protected?" asked Chiun.

"Look, Papasan, I have great respect for your traditions and all that, but I don't have time for riddles. Let's go."

With a courteous nod, Chiun followed the white man out into the night, past the cars and down the road. When they came to a gushing muddy sewer by the side of the road, Chiun assisted Van Riker's balance by tumbling him down into the ditch. Then he was upon the larger man with his feet, rolling him in the dirty water like a log.

Spitting blackness out of his mouth, Van Riker

gagged out, "What did you do that for? What did you do that for? First you tell me we have to walk and then you shove me in a ditch."

"Do you want to live?"

"Damned right, but not in a ditch."

"Ah well," sighed Chiun. He would have to make it simple for the great American scientist general. Chiun tried to think of some parable that would make it clearer. Something simple. Something that a child would understand.

Van Riker scrambled out of the sewer ditch, spitting and heaving.

"Once upon a time," said Chiun, "there was a delicate lotus whose beauty was known far and wide."

"Don't give me that Papasan routine. Why did you kick me in the ditch?"

Ah well, the courteous man tries many roads to understanding, thought Chiun. So he explained in a different way.

"If we were to drive to the church and monument, we would be stopped because all cars are stopped."

Van Riker nodded.

"You see the floating morning cannot sustain that which . . ."

"No, no, I got you the first time. Why the ditch?"

"Your suit acts like a beacon in the night."

"Why didn't you just tell me to change suits instead of kicking me into the ditch?"

"I did."

"But you didn't tell me why."

"One is not always sure a thimble will hold a

95

lake. Better that you know what, then later perhaps you can deal with why."

"All right, all right, all right."

They walked along the road, and when they were three hundred yards from the marshals' lights, Chiun signaled his charge down into the ditch at the left and then up the other side. They walked through crunching gravel for a while, and then Chiun signaled for Van Riker to halt.

"I'm okay. I can go on," said Van Riker.

"No, you can't. You are breathing wrong. Rest."

This time Van Riker did not argue. He waited. Then his eyes drifted upward, and he saw the night sky and the stars and was awed by the universe and his own smallness in it. Even the Cassandra would not be a speck on one of those stars out there.

"Magnificent," he said, mostly to himself. "How can one give thanks for such awesome magnificence?"

"You're welcome," said Chiun, somewhat surprised because he had not shown this strange fellow much, nor did he think this fellow would understand if he *did* see something impressive.

"The head of your organization said back in that hangar in Raleigh that you are the finest assassin in the world," said Van Riker, passing time until he got the signal to move again.

"Smith is not the head of my organization. I am the head of my organization, and I consider what he says silliness."

"How's that?"

"If he is not the finest assassin or even the second finest, how would he know? What do I know of your

Cassandra if I am not of the wisdom of your house of science? What do I know?"

"I see," said Van Riker. "That's the effectiveness of the Cassandra, you know. That we are dealing with people who understand what we have. If they didn't understand, then we wouldn't have a weapon."

Chiun placed a hand on Van Riker's chest. The breathing was good, but he was not ready to move, not for what Chiun wanted him to do.

"It is a bad weapon," said Chiun. "Of weapons I know, and the greatest is the mind. But this Cassandra is bad. If I had been advising the emperor, you never would have made this bad thing."

"We don't have emperors—we have presidents."

"An emperor is a president is a czar is a bishop is a king. If you call the man who rules you a lotus petal, still your lotus petal is an emperor, and your emperor made a mistake. That is a bad weapon."

"Why?" asked Van Riker, intrigued by the reasoning of the strange Oriental, who was supposed to have such awesome killing powers.

"The weapon is a threat. Correct? It is," Chiun went on, not waiting for a reply. "But the weapon is also a danger to your country. Otherwise you would not be here with me. You have created a weapon which has no direction. You might as well have created a tornado. No. A good weapon points only at the enemy."

"But the Cassandra had to be a superpowerful weapon to be an effective deterrent."

"Wrong. Your weapon had to be powerful in only one place, but you made it powerful in two, and

97

that is why it is bad weapon," said Chiun, pointing toward the lights of the monument. "There the weapon is in the wrong place . . . where it can hurt your own kingdom."

Chiun pointed to his own head. "Here, in the mind of your enemy, is the rightful place for your weapon. That is where it belongs—in his fear—because that is the only place it can really work. If it works at all."

"But we had to construct one, give enough accurate details to let them know we had one. How do you make them believe you have something you don't?"

"I am not in the habit of working out petty details for military failures," said Chiun. Then, feeling Van Riker's heart again, he added, "You are ready. Come."

They moved through the darkness across the plains, with Chiun leading Van Riker between gopher holes. When they came to a dark section, just before the lights at the ring of marshals' posts, Chiun told Van Riker not to move. To wait. To think about his breathing and the stars. But no matter what happened not to move.

Then Van Riker saw something he could hardly comprehend. The ancient figure in the dark kimono was before him, giving him instructions, and then he was not before him but part of the darkness. The lights at one federal marshal's outpost dimmed, and then another dimmed, but there was no sound, not even of a man being struck or of a man moving after being struck. There was the light, and then there was not the light. And while trying to see where Chiun was, he felt a tap on his back.

"Move," he heard the master of Sinanju say, and Van Riker walked straight ahead. As he passed the marshals' outposts, he saw that the men appeared to be sleeping.

"You didn't kill them, did you?"

"Look again."

Van Riker turned his head back toward the ring of marshals, and he saw the lights were now back on, and the marshals still stood with their backs to him and the Oriental, their guns cradled in their arms, their hips jutting out in relaxed slouch. They tossed pleasantries at each other—all as if they had been waiting there, bored and uninterrupted, for hours.

"How did you do that?"

"A mere nothing," said Chiun. "In our village children can do it."

"But how did you do it?"

"How did you build the Cassandra?"

"I couldn't explain just like that."

And Chiun smiled, and he saw the man understood. When they were close to the monument, Chiun insisted they wait. Even as the sky lightened, threatening morning sun, they waited in the open plain and no one seemed to spot them.

"Remo is back now," Chiun said. "We will go. Just walk with me."

"How do you know that?" asked Van Riker. "Then again, why should I doubt that you know it?"

A television news truck turned toward the spire of the church up ahead. A pack of men and women surrounded it and began unloading.

Van Riker saw Remo leap from the cab. There was a special silent grace in the man's movements, almost a reduction of all effort to a simple gliding motion that seemed familiar to Van Riker. Where had he seen it? In the Oriental, of course.

Remo saw Chiun and Van Riker inside the marshal's lines, and he started toward them. Just then a RIP guard with shotgun and six-shooter staggered to his feet, clinking hollowly as he walked across the aluminum beer cans sprinkled outside his sandbagged trench. "Halt there, you shits," he said to Chiun and Van Riker.

"Good morning," said Remo to the guard, who turned around into two fingers that shattered his nose. He went flew backward, horizontal at first. He saw the dark blue morning sky of Montana, then he saw the brown dirt prairie, and then he didn't see very much of anything at all.

"Very subtle," said Chiun, chiding. "You, Remo, are of a race of litterers. Beer cans, bodies. Litter."

"How's Van Riker?" asked Remo, seeing the scientist coated with dried mud.

"He shows a good primitive aptitude for martial concepts. Who knows what he might have been if his instincts had been encouraged in civilization."

"We must get to the Cassandra," said Van Riker. "And above all, please don't refer to it as the Cassandra. Call it the monument or something."

"Then let us hurry to the something," said Chiun, and he cackled and repeated the comment and cackled again and repeated the comment. As they walked through the crowd ripping open frozen din-

100

ners and rolling around in sugar-coated cereal and sucking the white fillings out of Twinkies, Chiun kept repeating his joke.

Van Riker was surprised to see the crowd part before him as people jumped from the path of the master of Sinanju, seemingly of their own volition. This was no Papasan, thought Van Riker.

"The great spirits have given us back our buffalo," cried Lynn Cosgrove, who had climbed to the top of the truck. "We are cleansing the land of the white poison which is in it."

A gust of wind caught her deerskin skirt and raised it, and seeing this, one of the braves threw a half-eaten Twinkie up between her beautiful white legs.

Remo, Chiun, and Van Riker pushed on. When they were within forty yards of the monument, Van Riker's broom began to crackle.

"Oh," said Van Riker. His knees became weak and wobbly, and Remo and Chiun had to hold him upright. He closed his eyes momentarily. Then he pushed aside a little shield at the base of the broom, which looked like a brand name. Beneath it was a needle. Van Riker looked at the needle, blinked and smiled vacantly at Remo, who noticed a sudden burst of wet darkness around Van Riker's fly.

"Is there a bathroom here?" asked Van Riker hoarsely.

"Too late," said Remo.

CHAPTER EIGHT

"It's going to blow." Van Riker's face was suddenly as damp as his trousers.

"Well, stop it," said Remo. "What do you think the government's been paying you for all these years? To stand around, peeing your pants and saying Gloryosky, Zero, the sky is falling?"

He looked toward Chiun for moral support. Chiun was shaking his head in disgust at Van Riker. The white-haired general was busy checking the needle on the broom again, tapping it with his right index finger.

"I can't stop it," the said. "The triggering mechanisms are all buried under the cap seal."

"So take off the cap seal, whatever that is," said Remo with all the outrage he thought was allowed to one whose logic is impeccable.

Van Riker had begun to regain his composure. He walked toward the giant black marble monument and pointed to the two bronze disks on its right side.

"Those are the cap seals," he said, "and we can't open them. They're machine fitted to tolerances of less than a hundred thousandth of an inch. After they were put in place, expanders opened inside, locking them on tight. Then the unit which opened the expanders was removed. The only way to open them is with a special sealing tool. And that's in Washington."

Remo smirked. "Chiun, open that for him, will you?"

"One side or both sides?"

"Will you two stop fooling? This is serious," Van Riker said. "We don't have the tools."

Chiun slowly raised his hands before his face. "These are tools, foolish toy-maker. One would think that after all these years your species would have learned to use them, too. Or is it because they do not break six months after you acquire them?"

"How much time do we have?" asked Remo.

Van Riker looked again at the hidden Geiger counter. "Fifteen minutes at the outside, I think. It's approaching a critical point. And then it can't be stopped. Everything blows." He paused. "You know . . . it's a strange feeling. I have this idea I should say 'Quick, everybody run, try to escape.' But in fifteen mintues, you couldn't get far enough to escape."

"Chiun, go open it, will you please?" asked Remo. "It'll be daylight pretty soon."

Chiun nodded and turned away from them.

"Those lights," said Van Riker. "Everybody's going to see him." He pointed to floodlights mounted atop two forty-foot poles, one at each end of the monument.

"We'll see," said Remo. He moved away from Van

Riker for a moment. Van Riker heard a wrenching sound and turned. As he looked, Remo was walking away from the nearest light stanchion. The pole had been twisted around in its deep concrete base, and now the light shone out onto the prairie, away from the monument.

"How . . . ?" started Van Riker.

"Do I ask you how to build a stupid missile?" asked Remo.

Outside the reach of the light, Chiun, dressed in his black nighttime robe, seemed like a supershadow as he bent over the first brass plate. His movements were obscured in darkness, but suddenly tremendous thudding sounds, like hammer meeting bell, tolled through the night.

Then there came another sound. It was the rumble of voices, and Remo realized it was drawing nearer.

"Kill the devil. Off the pig."

"White-eyed oppressor of the people."

Through the glare of the floodlights, directed once again toward the monument, came the RIP members, led by Dennis Petty. Twinkie cream still glittered on his face, matching the wild flashing of the whites of his eyes, as he stomped heavy-footed along in front of the rampaging RIP.

"There he is," yelled Petty to the crowd, pointing an accusing finger at Remo. "There's the traitor."

Remo stepped forward and went to meet them before they got too close to where Chiun was working. "Hi, fellas," he said. "How's the food?"

"Oh, white oppressor," moaned Petty. "Prepare to take your soul to that big chicken stand in the sky."

104

"What's the matter?" asked Remo. Behind him in the darkness, he could still hear Chiun's hands thudding against the metal caps. Remo knew he would have to keep these looneys away from Chiun while he worked. "What's the matter?" Remo repeated. "You got the food in the sacred buffalo—right?" he demanded pointing to the van. "I can tell," he said, "because you're wearing it all over your faces."

"You promised us provisions for the big battle."

"Right," said Remo.

"And you brought us Twinkies."

"And meat and milk and bread and cheese and vegetables and . . ."

"Ahah," said Petty. "Right. But no whiskey."

"No whiskey. No whiskey. No whiskey," roared the voices behind Petty. "And not even any beer, either," someone piped up.

"I thought it would be best," said Remo, "not to bring you the evil white man's firewater, since you now begin the most difficult struggle of your lives. Guarding your sacred lands and sacred heritage against the evil men from the big chief who art in Washington."

"Oh, fuck Washington."

"Screw the president."

"Down with the Joint Chiefs of Staff."

"Disband the House of Representatives."

"My soul rises from Wounded Elk," came a voice that could only have been Lynn Cosgrove's.

"Oh, shut up, dummy," yelled Petty. "You're as bad as white-eyes here. You went with him for the food and forgot the booze."

As he turned back toward Remo, Jerry Lupin stepped forward and hit Lynn Cosgrove with the butt of his rifle.

"Now what are you doing to do about it?" Petty demanded of Remo.

"Suppose I give each of you a buck," said Remo. "Then you can buy a couple of six packs."

"Beer is a cruel white hoax to deprive the red man of the firewater which is rightfully his."

Thump, thwack, crack . . . Chiun was still at work. Then there was silence. He must have opened it. Van Riker might need help dismantling the unit. It was time to disperse the party.

"All right, boys," called Remo. "Back to the Episcopal tepee. Keep your wigs warm."

"Racist joke!" screamed Petty. "Oh, my heart plummets like the dying dove."

"Fun's fun but enough's enough," said Remo. "Go home."

"Are you alone?" asked Petty.

"Right," said Remo. "Alone."

"Charge!" screamed Petty. Startled by his roar, the forty RIP members charged. Half got confused and charged in the wrong direction. Half of the remaining half charged into each other and started fighting among themselves. Only ten got moving in Remo's direction. The first one to reach him was Petty, whom Remo immediately put to sleep. Then Remo lifted Petty up over his head and tossed him at the nine other charging men.

"Leader sickum," said Remo. "He need heap big

medicine. You takeum him home and fixum him up. Or I breakum your asses. *Move* it!"

Shocked by Remo's terrible audacity in knocking out one of the forty men who had planned to kill him, the Indians retreated to plan their new strategy.

The new strategy revolved around some news they had gotten just that evening. Perkin Marlowe, the Hollywood star who was one 256th Indian if you could believe him, although no one had ever yet found a reason to, was on his way to Wounded Elk. He would set everything right. As Petty had pointed out, hadn't Marlowe just played a Mexican bandit who outwitted a whole army? If he could do that for mere Mexicans, who knew what wonderful things he could do for Indians?

As the RIP members trudged away, Remo turned back toward the monument to help Van Riker. But just then he heard another voice. Attracted by the noise, Jerry Candler of the *Globe* had slipped past the marshals' lines. He was standing now in the glare of the floodlight, only ten feet from Remo.

"Atrocities!" he screamed, pointing to Petty, who was being dragged away by the arms. "Atrocities!"

The tendons stuck out in his neck as he screamed, making him look like a chicken with a muscular neck. He was small, and his skin, which seemed stretched too tight, took on a vague fluorescence in the dazzling light.

"Oh, shut up," said Remo.

"Attica! Chile! San Francisco! And now Wounded Elk!" shouted Candler. "Well, I will expose this bestiality."

He looked hard at Remo, then swallowed and said, "Oh, my goodness. You've killed them."

"Killed who?"

Candler was looking past him now, into the darkness. Remo turned and followed his eyes. He saw that the caps had been removed from the access holes in the monument and Chiun had lifted two bodies out of the twin cylinders. Van Riker was scrambling down into the cylinder on the left. Only a few minutes remained of the fifteen Van Riker had given that part of the world.

"I think there's something wrong with your eyes," said Remo.

Candler sneered. "There's nothing wrong with my eyes. I can recognize murderous genocidal brutality when I see it."

Remo shook his head. "Oh, no. There's something wrong with your eyes. Something definitely wrong."

Impressed by his sincerity, Candler raised his right hand to his face and touched the sockets around both eyes. "What's wrong with my eyes?" he asked.

"They're open." Remo moved forward and tapped Jerry Candler on the back of the neck, and the reporter's eyes closed as if his eyelids were weighted. Remo let him drop to the ground, then went back to help Chiun and Van Riker.

Inside the cylinder he could hear Van Riker breathing heavily, occasionally grunting with the exertion.

"How's it going?" Remo asked.

"This is a nation of messers," said Chiun. "There were dead people in the cylinders."

"Oh, that's awful," said Remo. "The nerve of America, exposing you to death that way."

"Yes," agreed Chiun, "it is thoughtless."

They listened to more grunting, and then Van Riker's head emerged from the cylinder.

"Done," he said.

"It's disarmed?" asked Remo.

"Right. Harmless as a newborn babe." He lifted a twelve-inch part up over his head. It looked like some kind of transmission gear. "This out makes it safe."

He put the part down carefully and hoisted himself out of the hole. He stood there for a moment, brushing the dirt from his caked silver suit. "I just don't know how you got that seal off," he said the Chiun.

"You watched me. Now you should be able to do it."

Van Riker smiled weakly. "Science, I guess, does not know *all* the world's secrets."

"What you call science knows none of them," corrected Chiun.

"Get off there," said Remo. "We're going to have to put these bodies back."

He stepped toward the monument, and Van Riker quickly picked up the piece he'd removed from the Cassandra. "Careful not to touch this," he said. "It's highly radioactive. It could kill you in minutes."

He tossed it under a bush beside the monument, then climbed down from the marble.

He looked at the two bodies lying on the ground. "I though I would never see them again," he said.

"Your work?" asked Remo.

109

Van Riker nodded. "Not pleasant. But necessary."

Chiun nodded in agreement. Then he and Remo flipped the two dead men back into the cylinders and slid the barbell-shaped dual bronze cap over the holes.

"Now, listen, Van Riker. You're not going to have to open this again?"

"Right. Not again."

"Okay, Chiun," said Remo. "You can seal it tight."

He moved back to stand beside Van Riker, and both watched as Chiun scurried around the bronze cover.

He moved like an ant around the edges, his hands like flurries of yellow sparkle in a swirling wind. First one end, then the other. Total elapsed time: thirty seconds.

He stood up. "They are sealed. They will remain sealed."

"After things around here return to normal," Van Riker said mildly, "we'll have to open it up to make it operational again. But then we'll be sure to bring the special instruments from Washington."

"If you ever wish to open it again," corrected Chiun, "you would do well to bring high explosives. I said it is sealed."

They were interrupted by a moan. Jerry Candler rolled over on the ground, opened his eyes, and looked up. He shook his head, as if in disbelief, then saw Remo, Chiun, and Van Riker around the monument.

"Terrorists!" he shrieked. "Fascist executioners! Right-wing oppressors! Genocidal . . ."

"Who is this person?" asked Chiun aloud. "Why is he yelling at me?"

"I am part of the growing consciousness of America," screamed Candler hysterically.

"Make him part of the growing unconsciousness of America," Chiun suggested to Remo.

"I already did that," Remo said.

"You should have done it harder." To Candler, who was now lifting himself up off the ground, Chiun said, "Be gone, you. Before I seal your mouth with a stone."

Candler backed away slowly. "What'd you do with the bodies?"

"What bodies?" asked Remo.

Candler kept backing away, his voice growing louder as the distance between him and the monument increased.

"You haven't heard the last of this," he said. "I saw them. I saw the bodies. I know you killed two poor Indians. The world will know soon."

"Good," said Remo. "Everybody likes a little recognition for his work."

Candler slunk away.

CHAPTER NINE

Jonathan Bouchek was annoyed. He was starting to get pimples. Under his pancake makeup he could almost sense the little bastards first making tinies, and then getting bigger, creating little pools of pus under volcano-shaped lumps.

And all because of this frigging government!

Bouchek had been at the Wounded Elk siege for four days, and he had worn makeup twenty-four hours a day. It was especially important at night, since every night the concensus in the press tent was that tonight would be the night, that as soon as the government felt the press was asleep, it would unleash its massive manpower and armaments and massacre the small RIP encampment.

Night after night Bouchek stayed up and waited for the government to begin its brutal assault.

He had the scenario all mapped out in his mind. The government would send in tanks and armored personnel carriers. They were not fooling anyone by having just a second lieutenant, a corporal, and one jeep on the scene. All the reporters knew that the government had amassed thousands of men and tons of heavy equipment only a few miles away. They knew this for a fact because, they told each other, the government had to take that course. If the government allowed this Indian uprising to continue— why, all of middle America would soon be in the streets, marching along their neat lawns, driving one of their family's three cars, expressing their hatred of a government which had oppressed them so.

So the government would send in its armies. And Bouchek would be just one step ahead of everybody else. He had already found out that the National Guard second lieutenant on the scene wanted to be an anchorman. Bouchek had promised to make him one, and the second lieutenant had promised Bouchek the use of his jeep when the battle started.

Bouchek would ride into the war zone on the hood of the jeep. The cameras were already set up in the vehicle's back seat. In his mind's eye he could see it now.

Jonathan Bouchek, in profile, in three-quarter silhouette, his outline dark against the flashing light of government explosives and bombs, moving forward into battle to bring America the news as it happened. Edward R. Murrow, Elmer Davis, Fulton Lewis, Jr. —move aside. Here comes Jonathan Bouchek.

But the hated government had not yet charged, and now his pancake makeup was starting to crack at the folds in his face, as it did every morning after being on all night. And when it cracked, it itched. And he was afraid to scratch it because he knew that the moment he scratched it, the attack would start and he would not even be presentable on camera.

That would be just his luck. When the government went berserk against those sweet young men at Attica, Bouchek had been in the cafeteria having coffee. When the first ransom demand had been received in that San Francisco kidnapping, Bouchek had been three blocks away in a telephone booth, arguing with his office about his expense account.

This time he would not fail. He would not scratch his face, no matter how much it itched. If he got pimples—well, then he would get pimples and a dermatologist would solve that problem later. But for the time being, he would go ahead and suffer. It was all for America's benefit.

He looked around him at the sleepy press encampment in the early morning light. From his pocket he fished a small can of throat spray and worked over his tonsils for a few moments.

Another deadly dull night of no news. Back in New York, where they worried about things like that, they were soon going to start wondering if it was worthwhile having Bouchek on the scene if he was sending back so little news worthy of air time.

And then Bouchek heard some squealing and squeaking. It was Jerry Candler, running around, announcing that he was going to hold his own press conference in exactly thirty minutes and demanding that everyone attend.

Bouchek filed the ploy away for future use. Hold your own press conference. If there's no news, make some. That would get tube time. On the other hand, his network might not be happy with his becoming a newsmaker. He would have to sniff around to try to find out what their policy was about it.

Bouchek got a crewman with a hand camera and a sound technician, and after a wake-up cup of coffee, he followed the crowd of reporters to a point halfway between the line of marshals and the occupied church of Wounded Elk.

Candler had gotten himself a crowd. All the reporters were there. And there were a dozen or so of the RIP people, including Lynn Cosgrove, who was loudly insisting that she be called Burning Star. She nodded a lot while the talking was going on, and occasionally she moaned. Next to her was Dennis Petty, and next to him a minority-party United States senator.

Candler waved his hand for silence. "The pig government during the night brutally murdered two innocent Indians. I know because I was there. I saw their bodies. And I know they did nothing to warrant their deaths. They were unarmed. They were peacefully standing by the monument when they were killed brutally by five men wearing the uniforms of the United States Pig Army.

"The army will of course deny this. It may be denied all the way to the highest circles of Washington. But it happened. I saw it with my own eyes. And I write a column for the *New York Globe.*"

There was hardly a dry eye in the crowd when he had finished. But the onlookers didn't have a chance to subdue their emotions before that pushy reporter with the plaster head from one of the local New

York stations started asking questions. The nerve of him, though Jonathan Bouchek.

"Who were the two dead men?" the pushy reporter asked.

Candler looked surprised that anyone would care. He turned to Dennis Petty. "Who were the two martyrs?" he asked Petty.

Petty turned to Lynn Cosgrove and whispered, "You're good at this. Give me two Indian names."

"Uhhh, how about Bright Water and Treetop Tall," she whispered back.

Petty looked disgusted. "Bright Water's all right, but Treetop Tall sounds like something from the top forty." Stalling for time, he covered his eyes with his hand as if overcome by emotion. "Hurry up, bitch," he hissed.

"Sun That Never Sets," she said.

"Ohhhh," he groaned loudly. "My two companions who rode with me on the trail of elk and buffalo, Bright Water and Sun That Never Sets. Brutally massacred by the white-eyed devils, never to be seen again."

Reporters scribbled furiously. The minority-party senator was choked with grief. Tears ran down his face.

"That's terrible," he blubbered. "Awful. I think we should give everyone a thousand dollars."

"Tokenism," said Petty angrily. "We will not be satisfied with your government's filthy money. If it were an adequate amount, not just tokenism, we might talk."

"I think we should give everybody five thousand

dollars," said the Senator. "Reparations. To try to re-build the wounded soul of the brave red man."

"Oh, my soul bleeds at Wounded Elk," moaned Lynn Cosgrove.

"Knock off the commercials," hissed Petty. "I'm doing my own book, you know."

The press conference went on and on. Somebody handed Petty a rifle, and he danced around, waving it over his head.

Jonathan Bouchek was cheered up some. That footage was good, and it would enable him to drop the film of Jerry Candler making the initial charges. Why publicize a competing newsman?

Bouchek grabbed his small camera crew and moved away from the ring of reporters and the swelling number of Indians, who, now that they had awakened, were showing up to be on television.

Bouchek wet his right index finger on his tongue and smoothed the makeup in the creases of his face.

Then, as his camera rolled, he improvised: "Wounded Elk today was the scene of yet another massacre in its long, bloody history. Two Indian men—Bright Ocean . . . er, Water . . . and Sun That Never Rises—were shot down and killed by a company of soldiers here in the town that is being occupied by Indians protesting American oppression.

"The brutal slayings were witnessed by a number of people, among them a reporter for a major New York newspaper. Dennis Petty, chief of the Revolutionary Indian Party, said that the dead men were peaceably demonstrating when they were killed. He described them as decent, honest family men, both deeply involved in the Indian movement. He vowed never to rest until their deaths are avenged.

"And so the stage may once again be set for bloodshed at Wounded Elk."

Jonathan Bouchek would now know it until his office queried him on it, but his luck had again run true. While he was on camera, he missed a few other items from the press conference.

First, the minority-party senator promised a Senate investigation of the atrocity, which he called the worst genocidal act by America since its slaughter of Mexican patriots at the Alamo.

Second, Dennis Petty vowed that his RIP members would go on the warpath just as soon as Perkin Marlowe, the great actor and Indian and revolutionary leader, arrived upon the scene, which might be any minute.

"When he comes," Petty said, "we will seize our guns and march against the oppressors. Like a red wave, we will sweep this nation. We will win, or we will die," he said, adding, "which is going to be the title of my book about these atrocities."

Chiun and Van Riker had returned directly to the motel room.

Remo had drifted through the growing morning light into the press encampment and had wound up on the fringes of the news conference, trying not to be recognized, watching the lunatics harangue each other.

The press conference soon broke up, however. While publicity was nice, breakfast was better, Petty

118

had decided, remembering the cartons of Twinkies back at the church.

Lynn Cosgrove bumped against Remo as the crowd was breaking up.

"Hail, oh Burning Star, freer of the oppressed, guardian of the heritage and culture of the red people, Remo said.

"Fuck you, mother," spake Burning Star.

Remo shrugged.

"Fuck you and fuck your government and fuck your promises," she continued.

"You speak with fucked tongue," said Remo.

"Why didn't you get liquor?" she demanded.

"You were there. Why didn't you remember it?"

"I trusted you to lead the hunting party, and you failed me. Never again will I trust like that."

She jumped up and down. Her breasts moved solidly under the deerskin, and her red hair flashed around her face.

"Let's talk about it," Remo said. He took her arm and led her away to a TV van. Its doors were open, and there was no one inside. Remo lifted her in easily, followed her, and then locked the door from the inside.

"Your heart is not with the red man," said Burning Star.

"My heart is with you," said Remo, putting his right hand inside the neck of her dress and touching her left shoulder.

"You do not care that we are making history," said Burning Star.

"I'm more interesting in making you," said Remo.

He slid his hand behind her shoulder and found one of the three erogenously effective nerve clusters in her back.

Burning Star shuddered. "You are a fascist pig," she said.

"Never," said Remo. "I'm no fascist."

He squeezed her nerves again, and she fell forward into his arms. "Oh, great hunter," she said. "I am yours."

Remo gently settled her on the carpeted floor of the van, moving aside cartons of equipment, then put his lips near her earlobe.

"You sure?" he asked.

"Stop talking so much," she said.

And Remo made love to her as a giant aircraft whose side bore the red hammer and sickle swooped overhead, through the bright morning sky, like a silver bird.

CHAPTER TEN

When Remo returned to the room, he found Chiun sitting on the floor between the beds, staring at a small table lamp without a shade.

"Where's Van Riker?" Remo asked.

"I obtained for him a room next door," said Chiun. "Through there." He pointed to a connecting door.

"How'd you do that? This place is crammed full."

"It was nothing," said Chiun.

"Exactly how nothing?" Remo persisted.

Chiun sighed. "If you must insist upon checking me like a child, there was a reporter there . . . Walter something-or-other. I told him to go home if he wanted to live."

Remo started to speak, but Chiun said, "I did not touch him. I know your lust for secrecy." He turned again to look at the light bulb that glared brightly in the room.

"That was good work back there," Remo said.

Chiun was silent.

"I said, that was good work."

"Do you praise the light bulb for lighting?"

121

"What kind of a question is that?" asked Remo.

"A simple question. The kind you answer best."

"A lightbulb's supposed to light," said Remo.

"Aha," said Chiun, as if that solved everything.

"Right," said Remo. "And the rock melts before the water—but slowly."

"That is stupid," said Chiun.

"It is stupid whether you attack it or not," insisted Remo.

"Everything you do is stupid, no matter what anyone does."

"That is the secret of the wonder of it all," said Remo. "It's a negative positive."

"Oh, shut up," said Chiun.

As Remo went to the phone, he said, "We're done here, anyway. Just one more thing to do and then we're finished."

Chiun grunted, and Remo, regarding that as encouragement, continued while he dialed: "Yup, Cassandra's safe. It won't blow. There'll be an attack on those RIP people tomorrow by the Apowa, but that's no concern of ours. Hello, Smitty?"

"Well?" responded the lemon-wedge voice.

"Everything's okay," said Remo.

"Please explain *okay*."

"Van Riker defused the gadget. It's safe now."

"Good," said Smith. "Then you know what you have to do."

"Yeah, I know. He's kind of a nice old duck, though. Nothing like you."

"Sentimentality," said Smith, as if it were a grand jury indictment.

"Not really," said Remo. "When I do it, I'll just think of you. That'll make everything easy."

"Fine. Just do it."

Remo hung up, not quite as cheerful as he had been when he'd dialed. It seemed like a lousy way to start the day. But anything worth doing was worth doing quickly, he decided, as he strode to the connecting door to Van Riker's room. He opened it softly and heard a huffing sound. Then he stepped inside.

The bed was empty. In front of the window stood Van Riker, his back to Remo, doing deep knee bends.

He heard Remo and turned. "Morning," he said. "Exercises. Do them every morning. You exercise?"

"No," said Remo. "I'm beyond exercise."

Van Riker shook his head. "No way, fella. Nobody's beyond exercise. No matter what shape you're in, exercise can help. It can correct the trend toward dissolution."

"Dissolution," repeated Remo. "That's what I wanted to talk to you about."

"Well, listen," said Van Riker. "If you want, I could draft an exercise program that might help. Some calisthenics, a lot of slow-speed running . . . It'd start to straighten you out. How fast can you run?"

"What distance?" asked Remo.

"Say a mile."

"Three minutes," said Remo.

Van Riker looked pitying. "No. Really."

"Three minutes," Remo said.

"The world's record is just under four minutes," said Van Riker.

123

"That's not *my* world's record," said Remo.

"Have it your own way," said Van Riker, realizing that Remo did not share his passion for unnecessary movement. "Still, regular exercise would do wonders for you. Would you believe I'm fifty-six year old?"

"You've led a full life?"

"Yes," said the general.

"A happy one?" asked Remo, moving toward the bronze-skinned general.

"Pretty much. At least until the last couple of days. Defusing that thing this morning made my life happy again."

"Pleased with that, huh?" asked Remo, advancing another step.

"Yes, sir," said Van Riker. "Cassandra's safe now. About the only thing that could set it off would be some kind of big artillery hit."

"Artillery hit?" asked Remo.

"Sure. But it'd have to be a big one. A .155 millimeter, at least."

"Oh," said Remo, stopping where he stood. "A .155-millimeter shell could set it off?"

"I think so. But it'd have to be a good hit. Hey, where are you going?"

Over his shoulder Remo said, "To find a .155-millimeter cannon."

Chiun heard Remo speaking as he reentered the room.

"If you find a cannon, give it to the nuisance," Chiun said. "Maybe he can figure out another way to blow up his own country."

"Yuk, yuk," said Remo, stomping out into the morning warmth.

He was disgusted. All it would take for Cassandra to blow was a .155-millimeter cannon shell, and the Apowa had a .155-millimeter cannon, and they were going to use it on the town church and monument unless Remo delievered up the RIP members to them by tomorrow morning.

Remo found Brandt in the Big A supermarket, where he was chiding a group of women for squeezing toilet issue. The tissue was piled up almost to the ceiling.

"Why stop them?" asked Remo. "It's squeezably soft."

"Nonsense," said Brandt. "The only thing soft is the air inside the loosely wrapped package. The tissue itself feels like sandpaper."

Looking at the mammoth pile, Remo said, "You must sell a lot of toilet paper."

"Naaah," said Brandt. "But the guy I bought it from—now, *he* sold a lot of toilet paper." He laughed at his own joke, then asked, "Are you going to deliver?"

"Well, see, I wanted to talk to you about that."

"No time for big powwow," said Brandt. "I've got a business to run."

"Damn it, man, we're trying to save the world," said Remo.

"You save the world. All I want to save is this week's profits, and if I don't keep an eye on the checkout counters, the clerks'll loot me blind. I want those RIP slobs by tomorrow morning, or we're gonna blow that place up."

"How many of them do you want?"

"All of them," said Brandt.

"What are you going to do with them?"

"Give them a bath. Then hang them."

"That's against the law," said Remo.

"The hell with the law. Hey, you, leave that toilet paper alone! The hell with the law. They're ruining our church down there. And the law is letting them do it. That's bad enough. Worse is that they're ruining our image. People are watching this thing all over the world, and you know what they're thinking—so that's what Indians are like. We've gotta stop that. I want them all. The only good RIPper is a dead RIPper."

"How about just Petty and Cosgrove?"

"No way. Cosgrove'll dance around singing and give me a headache. Petty'll be so drunk he'll be hung before he sobers up. We want them all."

"Well, I'll try. But what if I can't? That cannon of yours probably won't shoot, anyway."

"Don't bet on it."

"How's a cannon that's never been fired going to shoot anything?"

"It's been fired," said Brandt.

"Oh."

"Every week for over a year."

"What for?" asked Remo.

"We picked it up from army surplus. We saw all this TV news jazz about riots and urban blight and stuff, and we figured it wouldn't take too long to get here and we were going to be ready for any blighters that tried to ruin our town.

"I'd love to see that cannon," said Remo cunningly.

"First you'll hear it. Tomorrow morning. Then if you're still around, I'll show it to you. Listen, you with the funny name, I want them all. All. All."

"Okay, you'll have them," said Remo.

"Stop squeezing that toilet paper!" yelled Brandt, turning from Remo and advancing menacingly on a sixty-year-old Indian woman in jeans and moccasins, who waited until he was close, then threw a four-roll pack at him and fled down the supermarket aisle.

Remo went out into the morning sun, disgusted with himself. Trying to get just one of the RIP people to the right place at the right time might tax his ingenuity; getting forty to deliver themselves to Brandt—and at daybreak, yet—was probably impossible.

Remo moved into a small municipal park with neatly clipped grass and manicured flowers in geometric patterns, which surrounded a large wooden monument praising the Apowa's veterans. He sat down on a bench to think it out.

The park, like the Big A supermarket, was near the edge of the mesa, and a half-mile away, well below the elevated village, Remo could see the Wounded Elk monument and the church.

Why shouldn't the Apowa be angry? They were a people with pride—pride in themselves, pride in their country. The park he sat in was a memorial to wars fought and died in. Little Indian children played among ceremonial machine guns mounted in concrete, old artillery pieces half-buried in the ground, a tank without treads—and also without graffiti. The children's happy voices hung shrilly in the clear air.

And down there at the church were the RIP ragtags. Hustlers without pride in themselves—and justifiably so. Ripoff artists who were conning the press and the government and someday, perhaps, would even convince the public. At first the public would think they were crazy. But the power of the press is cumulative, and night after night of news about oppression and the brave band of Indian liberators would cause even the strongest minds to lose track of what was really true. That was what at times made the press a threat to the country. Like water on rock, it could wear away traditions, beliefs, standards, and melt everything down in a stew of relativism until there were no absolutes, and the only god was the great savior Ad Hoc.

Remo listened to the children playing happily among the instruments of past wars.

Those kids deserved to live, even if only to be allowed to die later on for something that would be worth their lives. It was absurd to allow them to die because of a flurry of rage against the RIP garbage touched off a skilling nuclear exposion.

Remo stood up and walked away from the park with its beautiful high-ground command of the monument and the church and the highway, and headed back toward his motel. He would deliver the RIP members to Brandt. Somehow.

When Remo got back to his motel, he found Lynn Cosgrove, squatting in front of his door. She looked up at him with supplicant eyes. "You have despoiled me, white man," she said.

"Yeah, sure."

"You have made of me a Sacajawea."

"Whatever you say."

"I am ruined, made worthless by the power of your evil."

"Right, right."

"There is nothing left for me but to subject myself to a life of slavery at your blood-stained hands."

"Terrific, sweetheart, but not right now."

"I am an outcast among my own people. I will be your slave."

"Go eat a Twinkie."

"Goddamn it, Remo, screw me."

She jumped to her feet and began stamping up and down.

Remo touched a spot under her ear, near her throat, and she changed from hissing panther to purring tabby. "Oooooooh," she moaned.

"Yes, indeed," said Remo. "Look, I'm going to be very busy today. But tonight, say three A.M., I'll meet you at the church.

"Oooooooh."

"You understand? Three A.M. at the church."

"Oooooooh. Yes. Oooooooh."

Remo released his light touch. "Okay, go away now."

"I go, master. This worthless creature leaves because she lives only to do your will."

She walked away, and Remo watched her leave. Three A.M. at the church. He had a plan, and it might just get the RIP band up to the town.

CHAPTER ELEVEN

Chiun was not in the room, but Van Riker was. He was sitting in a chair watching a late morning talk show that featured two sociologists and the minority-party senator who had been at Jerry Candler's press conference. They were talking abou the deep sociological significance of the Wounded Elk uprising.

Van Riker looked away from the TV as Remo entered.

"I've been away from America too long," he said. "Is everybody this nuts?"

"No," said Remo. "Only the brightest ones. The average people are still pretty sane."

"Thank God for that!" said Van Riker, running a hand down his well-shaved tan cheek. "Listen to this crap. Will you just listen to it?"

Remo sat lightly on the edge of the bed and watched as one sociologist—black—said that the events in Wounded Elk were all that could be expected when a people had been enslaved for so long. "Eventually they must rise up against the ruling class," he said. "This is the significance of what

131

is happening in Wounded Elk. Poor, indigent, down-trodden Indians are rebelling against a government whose Indian policy borders, at best, on fascism and genocide. There is a lesson here for all minority peoples."

Yeah, thought Remo, and there's another lesson up at the Big A supermarket, where the Apowas shop and worry about nonsense like squeezing the toilet paper in a town where they live like human beings, a town they built with their own sweat.

It consoled him somewhat to realize that probably not a soul up there in the Apowa village was watching the show. If any one was, by chance, he was probably rolling on the floor, laughing.

The second sociologist—white—was now asking to be flayed. He predicted even higher levels of violence, and his eyes glinted wildly and spittle appeared at the corner of his mouth. He was a man in the throes of passion, ecstatic at the thought of someone attacking whites.

Then came the minorty-party senator. "Political solutions have failed. The administration has refused to support my plan to give everybody ten thousand dollars in reparations. So even though I support the uprising one thousand percent, I must now wash my hands of it. The higher levels of violence that must now come will not be on my conscience but on the conscience of those in Washington who turned a deaf ear to the pleas of those poor Indians."

The moderator was a slim blond man with a penchant for laughing at himself. This, Remo thought, was of a piece with the philosophy of the French general who once asked where the people were going so he could hurry up and lead them there.

The moderator now asked what kind of men were occupying the massacre site at Wounded Elk.

"Average, every-day Indians," said the senator. "Red brothers who have labored to try to build normal lives despite terrible deprivation and hardship."

Van Riker stood up angrily. "Who and what are they talking about? Is there another Wounded Elk somewhere that we don't know about?"

"General, you *have* been away from the country too long. The black one, you see—he's for all kind of violence by everybody. He wants to make violence as American as apple pie because it excuses violence when it's used to promote something he believes in.

"The white one, well—he's for violence because he thinks he ought to be punished for going to an Ivy League school. It never occurred to him that he went to an Ivy League school because his folks worked and because he had the brains to make it. Somehow, he's gotten the idea that his education was extracted forcibly from somebody who thinks that 'he do' is proper English."

"And the senator?" asked Van Riker.

Remo shrugged. "He's just a dumb shit."

"You know, that's the most perceptive social analysis I've ever heard," said Van Riker.

"I owe it all the Chiun," said Remo. "By the way, he'll be coming back soon. I don't think he'll appreciate your watching his television set."

Van Riker turned the set off. "It's all right. I'm

going for a walk, anyway. Oh, it'll be nice to get to the Bahamas again. As soon as this blows over and the AEC crews can come and put Cassandra back together again."

"Have a nice walk," said Remo.

Van Riker disappeared through the connecting door into his own room, and Remo flopped back onto the bed, debating whether or not to exercise.

He decided he would, since he hadn't had a good workout for over a week. Where would he exercise today? London? Paris? Algiers? San Francisco? Dayton, Ohio? White Plains, New York? None of them excited him today.

Wait. There was a little town in the Berkshire Mountains where Chiun had been receiving mail at a post office box. He and Remo had driven up there to collect the mail one day after it had been lying around for months and the post office had threatened to close the box down. Chiun had been expecting job offers and was disappointed because the letters did not contain even one offer of temporary employment. But he stolidly refused Remo's suggestion to throw the letters away.

What was that town? Right. Pittsfield, Massachusetts. Right. He remembered now. And there was a pond near there. And a Girl Scout camp where the girls sang terrible songs terribly at terrible hours of the day and night. And there was a flautist who walked out to the edge of the pond most mornings to play and to shame the very birds.

Remo pictured it now. Pittsfield. He closed his eyes. The pond. He put his foot on the edge of the

134

water. He moved slowly to his right, along the water's edge, gliding. It was night and dark, and he glided along the water's edge, moving swiftly but lightly, trying not to make a sound.

In his mind he heard his foot touch a twig and snap it. Mentally he criticized himself. He began to run faster, skipping along the pond's edge, setting feet lightly on wooden docks when they got in his way, occasionally running across the bows of anchored boats. Move, move. His speed increased. He could feel a little perspiration forming on his neck. He checked his senses. His heartbeat was increasing. Good. No workout was any good unless the heartbeat accelerated. He felt a cold breeze blow off the water onto his forehead.

He was racing now at full speed. He was halfway around the pond. He had forgotten something—he had failed to move more blood into his legs. He lay there, willing the blood into his lower extremities, and he felt them flush and heat.

Good. He kept moving. He slowed down at the Girl Scout camp, stealthily, moving darkly through the dark night. With his hands he found and ripped out the wires of their public-address system, then continued on his way.

It was another ten minutes before he returned to his starting point.

His heart was beating strongly; his respiration was up to twelve breaths a minute from its usual seven. There was a faint trace of perspiration on his neck, under his chin, and at his right temple.

Great, thought Remo, gulping air, moving his heartbeat down and his respiration back to normal. What a great workout. What a beautiful evening in Pittsfield, Massachusetts.

The front door opened, and Chiun entered. He paused in the doorway and looked at Remo lying on the bed.

"Why are you perspiring?"

"I was just working out, Little Father," said Remo.

"It is about time you did something but lie on your back in bed," said Chiun.

"Thank you. I aim to please."

Chiun stepped inside the room, then turned to usher someone else in.

"Remo, I want you to meet this nice man I just met. He has a foolish name, but he is a nice man."

The fat man wobbled into the room and looked at Remo through piercing electric eyes that looked like chips of blue anthracite, set in a face of uncooked muffin dough.

"What is your name?" asked Remo.

"Valashnikov."

"That's right," Chiun said. "That is his name. But you can call him comrade. He told me everyone can call him comrade. Comrade, this is my son, Remo." He moved closer to Valashnikov and pretended to whisper but spoke loudly enough so that Remo could hear. "He isn't really my son, but I say that to make him feel adequate."

"It is pleasure to meet you," said Valashnikov to Remo, who was still lying on the bed.

"See," said Chiun. "See. Isn't he pleasant? He

136

says hello. Isn't he nice? Don't you like him? Don't you like him better than some emperors we know?"

At this moment Remo had decided he hated Valashnikov worse than anyone he had ever met or even heard of. A Russian. Wounded Elk hadn't been a bad enough mess. Now the Russians were arriving to turn it into an international debacle.

"What are you doing here, Valashnikov?" asked Remo.

"I am cultural attaché to Russian Embassy."

"And you came out here to find culture?"

"I am in charge of the Russian-American friendship through the music. I come to hear the authentic Indian music. Mother Russia is interested in such things."

"Russia is interested in a lot of things, Remo," said Chiun. "Why, do you know that they even treat assassins like honored people instead of the way some people we know treat them?"

"That's great," Remo said without enthusiasm.

Valashnikov entered the room and sat down heavily on the stool in front of the dresser.

"Is truth," he said. Russia understands principle of using different skills the different people have. We honor assassins. Particularly those who have done the labor for many years without the reward."

He looked at Remo searchingly. Remo looked at Chiun, whose eyes were rolled upward in a gesture of humility and unconcern. Remo looked disgusted. So Valashnikov was just a recruiting agent; Remo would have preferred it if he *had* been a spy.

And Remo was getting annoyed with Chiun's job-hunting. It was one thing to expect America to fold and collapse by three o'clock the next afternoon, but looking around to other countries for work . . . why, that was wrong. And Remo's thinking it was wrong was the only proof he ever needed that he was not the master of Sinanju and never could be. Chiun was an assassin; all sides were the same to him as long as they paid on time. Remo was a patriot; he wished to use his skills for no one but America. He would make no moral judgment about which attitude was better. It was just that he and Chiun were different.

"Any assassin who came to work for Mother Russia would find warm welcome," said Valashnikov. He looked to Chiun. "High honors," he said. He looked to Remo. "Much money."

"Company car?" asked Remo.

"Yes," said Valashnikov eagerly. "Not only that. But apartment. Two bedrooms. Right near Moscow. Seventeen-inch television set. Your own radio. Charge account at Gumm's."

He smiled suddenly, and just as suddenly the smile vanished. "I understand that is what your leaders call offer you can't refuse."

"Isn't he a nice man, Remo?" asked Chiun. "Don't you like him?"

"He's sweet, Little Father, and so are you. I hope you'll be very happy together." He got up from the bed. "I'm going for a walk. The idea of my own seventeen inch television set has staggered me. I need air to clear my head."

Remo walked outside, resolved to put the Russian out of his mind for a while. He had other problems.

The Apowa tribesmen were ready to blow up the monument and the church with a .155 millimeter cannon unless Remo delivered the RIP gang. Now how was Remo going to get them all to the Big A?

That was problem number one. And if Remo failed, Brandt would use his cannon and more than likely wipe out America by setting off the Cassandra.

Against that the Russian problem paled into insignificance. He would let Chiun continue negotiating with Valashnikov for a pure gold offer to go to Russia. When push came to shove, Remo could end those negotiations in a flash. He had a special secret weapon that Chiun didn't know about.

The idea of the Russians sending a recruiter all this distance to try to snatch up Chiun!

And then Remo found he had another problem. Walking along the dirt road leading from the motel toward the press compound, he met Van Riker. The general was striding crisply along the street at a hundred twenty steps per minute. He saw Remo, smiled and asked, "Where's the Oriental?"

"He's back in his room being propositioned by a Russian agent," said Remo airily.

Van Riker looked surprised, not sure whether or not to believe Remo. Finally he said, "Oh? Who?"

"Valash-something," said Remo.

Van Riker's face turned pale under his tan. "Tell me. Did he say Valashnikov?"

"Yeah, that's it."

"Oh, my God," said Van Riker.

"What's the problem?"

"He was a Russian intelligence officer. His job was

to find the Cassandra. When he failed, he was exiled. And now he's back.' After all these years. And this time, he's found it."

"I don't think so," said Remo. "I really think he just came to offer Chiun a job."

"Maybe he's doing that, too. But he came here because of the Cassandra. He knows it's here."

"So what?"

"Then its whole value is gone," said Van Riker. "If its location is known, an enemy can knock it out on the first strike. And we've lost our destroy-in-death capability."

"If he *knew* it was here, would he have come here?" asked Remo.

"Hmmmm," Van Riker reflected. "You're right, you know. He suspects, but he's not sure."

"All right," said Remo. "Then just play dumb. Leave him to me."

He walked away from Van Riker, telling himself he would have to call Smith that afternoon for more instructions on how to deal with the Russian. Killing him might be simple, but it would infuriate Chiun, who would think Remo did it only to prevent Chiun's taking the Russian offer.

Problems, problems, problems.

CHAPTER TWELVE

Smith, as usual, had been analytical. No, it would not do for Remo to kill Valashnikov because if the Russians did not now know the location of the Cassandra, Valashnikov's sudden death would be all the proof they needed that the missile was at Wounded Elk.

There were, if Remo would but remember, two goals to his assignment. The first and most important was to make sure that the Cassandra was not detonated. Remo was still working on that one and should concentrate on it. Keeping the Russians from finding out Cassandra's location was only a secondary goal ... a poor second.

Smith had gone on in this fashion for nine minutes before Remo finally stopped him by hanging up. Remo had done what he had to do: alert Smith. He would leave the problem of Valashnikov to him now.

Remo's own problem was getting the RIP contingent up to the village of Wounded Elk, and he felt pretty good about that. He had a plan. He whistled happily as he trotted along the dark road toward the RIP encampment in the Episcopal church. His plan would work. It would be a snap. The thinking man won every time.

"Who goes there?"

Oooops. If he didn't want to be noticed, he decided, he had better stop whistling.

He froze. He was dressed in black, and his dark shape blended with the darkness. The guard, ten feet away, looked around carefully but saw nothing. He wheeled suspiciously around and looked behind him. Still he saw nothing. Suspicious to the last, he peered again into the darkness toward Remo, but finally he put down his rifle and resumed leaning on it.

Remo moved off softly past the guard, continuing toward the church.

It *would* be easy.

The RIP people wanted booze. Remo would tell them he had found some. He would load them all into the back of the sacred buffalo TV van, which the TV crew had been afraid to demand back, and he would drive them all up to Brandt's store. And that would be that.

Brilliant, Remo.

Up ahead, the church glared with light, the only bright spot in a black night. Remo heard singing, the voices soft at first, then louder as he drew nearer.

"Back your ass against the wall . . . Here I come . . ."

They were singing dirty songs. And loud, Remo realized as he drew even nearer.

"I know a girl who lives on the hill. What she won't do, her sister will. Sound off . . ."

They were screaming now. Well, at least he wouldn't have to wake them. As Remo paused at the foot of the church steps, he heard a sound: "Psssst. White-eyes."

He turned toward the hedges at the left side of the church steps.

"Psssst. In here."

He stepped forward and heard a rustling sound.

"You're late."

He looked down. Lying on the ground, her buckskin shirt up around her hips, was Lynn Cosgrove. But she wasn't alone. Lying beside her, apparently sleeping, was Jerry Lupin. He was naked.

"Late for what? Cover yourself up. That's indecent."

"You said you'd be here at three. It's five after. The human body is never indecent. It is glorious in all its rampant sexuality. Besides, I'm your slave. You have violated me and stolen my honor. I am yours to do with as you will. So do with me. Please! I've been waiting."

"Waiting? With him?" asked Remo, pointing to Lupin.

Lynn Cosgrove smiled. "I found out it's good with anybody. Anybody at all."

"Good," said Remo. "Stick with him."

"You promised," she screamed.

"You know you can't trust a white man," Remo said.

"You can't trust anyone over thirty," she said.

"You can't trust a reactionary," he said.

"You can't trust a man," she said. "A sexist, mind-

143

less pig. I'm not your object, you know. I'm a human being, with human feelings."

"You could have fooled me," Remo said.

"Are you going to rape me?"

"No."

"You must. You have to rape me."

"Why must I?" asked Remo.

"Because I need it."

"Is that all I am to you? A sex object?"

"That's irrelevant. Rape me."

"No," said Remo.

"Filthy pig," she hissed. "I will never again waste my body on a man not worthy of the gift."

Remo heard her rustling around in the grass. Then he heard her voice. "Come on. Wake up. I need it again. Wake up there, you."

Remo felt like rooting the unconscious Jerry Lupin on. At least sex might keep her quiet—something that seemed beyond the reach of any other technique.

The roar from the church was deafening.

"We shall overcome some day . . .

Umgawagawa. Umgawagawa."

Remo hopped up the stairs and walked in through the open door.

The interior of the church looked like a Bowery corner on a Sunday morning. Some people slept sitting up; others slept lying down on the floor and on the pews. The altar trays and cloths had been swiped off onto the floor, and the altar was being used as a bar. It was stacked full of every imaginable type of liquor, and Dennis Petty was presiding as bartender while also leading the singing.

He saw Remo and waved. "Hey, sing with us," he called.

"We shall not be moved," he roared, waving a full tumbler of whiskey over his head, his words echoed by a dozen people, who were still able to move their lips for something other than swallowing.

"By the shores of Gitchee Goomee," yelled Remo.

"We shall overcome . . . some . . . day," roared Petty.

"By the old Moulmein Pagoda," yelled Remo.

"Those ain't the words," said Petty.

"Where'd you get the booze?" asked Remo in disgust.

Petty tapped his forehead with his right index finger. "We got friend, wise ass. Not just you with your Twinkies."

"Name one friend you've got," challenged Remo.

"Perkin Marlowe, that's who," said Petty.

"He sent you this booze?"

"Right. A whole truckful."

"Is he coming?" asked Remo. "I hope he's coming here. I just hope he's coming here. I want to see him. I hope he's coming."

"Who cares if he's coming?" yelled Petty. "We got the booze. And there's more coming tomorrow. We shall overcome . . . this day . . . and the next day . . . and the next day. And as long as the booze holds out."

This time there were only four or five voices accompanying his. Everyone else had collapsed. Remo looked around at the interior of the church. So much for well-laid plans. It would take a moving company to haul this load of human garbage up to the Apowa village on time.

He thought again of just dragging along Petty and Lynn Cosgrove. But Brandt wouldn't settle for them.

The decision was simple. Remo was going to have to find that .155 millimeter cannon.

Van Riker slept as Remo made his way through the night to the Apowa Village, but the general was not alone. Another figure was in Van Riker's room. A hulk of a man, sitting in a chair next to Van Riker's bed, smoking cigarette after cigarette, the butts pinched near the filter by all five fingers of his right hand. His left hand cradled a pistol on his lap. The man studied Van Riker's tanned face in the dim light of the night-light near the bathroom.

Van Riker's sleep had been troubled. He had been upset when Remo had told him that Valashnikov had arrived at Wounded Elk. But when Van Riker had gone to Chiun's room, neither Chiun or Valashnikov had been there.

The general had waited for hours, struggling to decide whether he should call Washington. But whom could he call? What could he say? No one in Washington knew of the Cassandra, and few had even heard of General Van Riker. Call the FBI? They would start a dossier on Van Riker as a crank. The CIA? They would make a careful note to discuss it at next month's briefing, five days after some clerk leaked it to Jack Anderson.

Finally Van Riker returned to his own room and fell asleep, but his sleep was restless, haunted by visions of a wave of Russian missiles launched at America on a preemptive first strike of war. And a half-dozen of those missiles were aimed at Wounded Elk, to destroy America's best single hope of keeping the world from war. Once Valashnikov was sure of the location of the Cassandra, it would be easy for the Russians. Valashnikov wouldn't even have to plant a homing device near the monument. All the Russians would need would be a geography book.

Van Riker's eyes flicked in sleep, moving back and forth as he saw the Montana hills exploding with nuclear color and America's great cities being leveled by Russian missiles.

And then he was awake. In his mind he had seen a red fireball of destruction rising over Baltimore. Now as he opened his eyes, he saw a faint red glow in his room. For a moment he was frightened, but then he realized that the red ball was only the head of a lit cigarette. Someone was sitting by his bed.

"Valashnikov?"

"Yes, General," come the heavily accented voice. "It is pleasure after all these years."

"How long has it been?"

"Ten years," said Valashnikov, stabbing his cigarette out in an ashtray. "Ten years wasted because the idiotic NKVD could not tell difference in translation between *tan* and *Negro*. Well, no matter . . . I am here now, and so are you. Is all that matters."

"I won't tell you anything," said Van Riker.

"You don't have to," said Valashnikov. "The fact you are here tells me all I need to know. If you are here, Cassandra is here. Mother Russia needs no other knowledge."

Van Riker sat up slowly in bed. Outside the window the blackness of night was growing lighter. Dawn would come soon.

"That's doesn't seem likely," he told Valashnikov. "If it were that simple, why did you come here?"

"Forgive me, General," Valashnikov said. "For a human reason—to gloat. You have cursed my life for ten years. You and that infernal device of yours. But now I have won. I came so you could know the feelings I have carried in me for ten years. The feelings of loser." He laughed. "I suppose it seems foolish to you, but I wanted you to know what you did to me."

"Are you going to kill me?" asked Van Riker.

Valashnikov laughed again, a hard, brittle laugh. "Kill you? Kill you? After all these years? No, General, I am going to let you . . . how do you Americans say it? . . . to stew in the juice?"

"I'll move Cassandra and set it up elsewhere."

"It will take you months. You know and I know that months will be too late. It will be seen. You were able once to build it in secret because we not know it existed. No more do you have that luxury."

"I'll . . ." Van Riker said and then stopped because he could think of no other threat, nothing that might frighten Valashnikov.

Valashnikov stood up. "Good, General. At least you have not tried to lie to me again. You may go back to sleep now. You should sleep with the bliss of knowing you have doomed your nation."

He put his gun in his jacket pocket. "Sleep tight,"
148

he said. "Hahahahaha." As he left the room through the front door, the long peal of laughter hung in the air behind him.

Van Riker sat there in bed, thinking. Then he got up, turned on the light, and went to the telephone.

There was one person who could help. One person he could call.

Dr. Harold W. Smith, at the Folcroft Sanitarium.

CHAPTER THIRTEEN

The sun was minutes short of rising when Remo got to the Apowa village high on the hill overlooking the mob of reporters, marshals, and bogus Indians out on the Montana prairie.

Remo paused on the edge of the mesa and looked down. Below him, beside the road that led to the Apowa village, stood the church housing the Revolutionary Indian Party and the bronze and marble monument housing the Casandra.

Remo turned and trotted toward the Apowa town.

It was pushing five thirty now, he knew, and he didn't have much time left to stop that .155 millimeter cannon from blowing up the monument and detonating the Cassandra.

For a moment he allowed himself to consider what would happen if the Cassandra went off. He would die. So would Chiun. That thought shook him a little, since the idea of Chiun's dying seemed unbelievable, as unbelievable as the idea repealing the law of gravity or stopping some other force of nature.

But Cassandra's power was beyond them to resist.

Death. A strange thing. And Remo decided he didn't like it. He wondered if that was the way all the people he had killed had felt. The next time he killed somebody, he would have to ask him what he was thinking about. That is, if there *was* a next time.

Brandt had thought he was smart, hiding the cannon. But Remo had thought the problem through, and the solution had come to him in a burst of inspiration. Why not hide the cannon out in the open? Where else but in the park? The park, with its collection of machine guns and artillery and the kids playing harmlessly around them. The park with its beautiful high-ground view of the church and the monument and the highway. All he had to do was go to the park and find a working .155 millimeter cannon.

That was all he had to do.

But it was too much. Remo went through the park carefully, checking each and every weapon. None of them was the potentially dangerous cannon. There were submachine guns that didn't fire. Bozookas that wouldn't fire. Mortars that couldn't fire. Cannons that had never fired. But there was no working cannon that could level the church, destroy the monument, and detonate the Cassandra.

Only twelve minutes left, and Remo was lost. He didn't even know where Brandt lived so he could get to his house in time to bleed the information on the cannon's location from him. He was without ideas and without prospects.

The village around him was slowly starting to come alive. People were moving quietly along the streets.

Remo watched them. America on its way to work. God-fearing, hard-working America.

He watched God-fearing, hard-working America idly for a moment from his perch on the park bench. Then he thought of something. Who went to work at five thirty A.M.? And these were all young men. Braves. And they all seemed to be going in the same direction.

It was no hope at all, but it was his only hope. Remo fell in with the small groups moving past the park, up toward the north. He walked fast, occasionally passing one of the groups but still able to follow the one just ahead.

Then he realized where they were going. The Big A supermarket!

Remo arrived there just a few minutes before six. Even though it was two hours before opening time, the interior of the store was already brightly lighted. Inside Remo could see Brandt. He was talking to a group of twenty young men, and more young men were arriving each minute, entering through the unlocked, pressure-operated front doors.

As the doors opened and closed, Remo could hear fragments of what Brandt was saying: ". . . supposed to be here . . . have to get rid of them ourselves . . . did you work out coordinates?"

The group which had now swelled to forty men, followed Brandt to one side of the store. As Remo watched, they fell onto the enormous display of toilet tissue, carrying the rolls away, first four-roll packages, then boxes, and then cartons, finally baring, under the protective mound of paper, the cannon.

Remo understood why Brandt had gotten so upset when the women shoppers had hovered around the display. Sometime after the RIP had occupied the church, he had moved the cannon into the store from wherever its hiding place had been.

What a dumb place to store a cannon. So dumb, Remo almost hadn't found it.

Now all he had to do was stop it from being fired, hopefully without hurting anybody. The Apowa were, after all, his kind of people, and Remo's sympathies lay with putting a shell into the church.

Brandt now was supervising as the Indians wheeled the cannon out of a small chicken-wire shed. The cannon was a big one. The top of its muzzle reached higher than a man's head.

Figuring that there had to be a side door to wheel it out through, Remo trotted around the low cinder-block building and found the wide delivery doors at the back. He found something else, too—the main power lines for the building. Remo looked for a fuse box on the outside wall but could not find one. The twin power lines came from utility poles to a spot about twelve feet up on the wall. They were connected there to heavy porcelain insulated mountings and then went through holes in the masonry wall into the building.

Remo leaped up and grabbed one of the insulators with his left hand. This would be tricky. He didn't understand electricity, so he took pains to figure it out carefully. If he just sliced one of the electric wires while he was touching the wall or the ground, he would be grounded and the jolt of electricity would pass through and probably kill him. Suppose he had worn his sneakers? Stupid, that wouldn't matter, he decided. But he wished he had them. Anyway, he had to cut the wire without being grounded.

Remo dropped back to the blacktop of the loading area. He stood under the twin wires, then crouched and leaped straight up.

At the top of his leap, he windmilled his right hand around his body and over his head. The hand hit the heavy insulated cable and sliced through it, separating the wire into two parts.

Remo, still off the ground, felt nothing but a faint tingle on the side of his hand. He landed lightly and danced out of the way of the severed section of cable, that writhed about the ground like an electric snake, sparking and spitting out its evil juice.

Remo poised himself, then leaped again and slammed his hand through the second wire. It too split and hit the ground with a splashing surge of electricity.

As soon as he landed, Remo was moving away from the spitting wires. He heard shouts from the supermarket.

"What the hell's going on?"

"Somebody go look at that fuse box."

He had to work fast now. He went back around the front of the store just as a faint hint of pink was beginning to lighten the eastern sky. The automatic doors in front of the market no longer worked, and Remo had to force them open. Then he was inside, in the darkness, moving among the Indians, who had

154

stopped wheeling the cannon and were waiting for the lights to come back on.

He moved in close and felt the cold polished steel of the barrel over his head. He tested the metal with his fingers and gave it exploratory taps with the sides of his hands. There were always weak spots in a machine, and a cannon was a machine. Chiun said there was always a spot where vibrations would bring it apart. He worked faster now, hitting the heels of his hands against the metal. And then he found it—a place that did not vibrate under his hands with the same dull hum as the other spots on the barrel.

Remo wrapped his hand around that spot on the barrel. Then from below, he began to swing his hands up and over his head, smashing hand against steel. It was rhythm—the pounding, left hand after right hand, left hand after right hand. in precise time, almost like a metronome. It filled the supermarket with dull bongs.

"Who's making that racket?" somebody nearby yelled.

"Cannon inspector," Remo answered.

Somebody else chuckled.

Then suddenly Remo, satisfied the metal now was vibrating in time with the thuds of his hands, changed the rhythm into a staccato series of smashes. The barrel of the cannon seemed to groan in pain. Remo stopped and slowly began to move toward the front door.

From the back of the store he heard a voice. Brandt's. "Damned wires come loose from the building somehow. I've some some lights here. Everybody get one."

Men surged toward Brandt and took the battery-operated lights he held in his arms. Then they walked back toward the cannon, lights on and swinging in front of them, and illuminated the huge weapon.

"What the hell?" said someone.

"I'll be a son of a bitch," said Brandt.

The cannon stood there as it had before, but now its barrel, instead of pointing ceilingward in phallic pride, drooped impotently toward the floor of the store, like a shriveled stalk of celery.

Remo was already outside, trotting toward the road to get back to his other main problem—Valashnikov.

But he was not fast enough. The enraged Brandt had gone to the window to look outside, and in the early morning light, he saw Remo trotting away.

"Damn it," he said. "Dirty, double-dealing, double-crosser." He slammed his right fist into his left palm. "If you think we're done, funny name, you've got another think coming."

CHAPTER FOURTEEN

General Van Riker had been successful. This, Valashnikov realized when the telephone rang in his room at the motel. On the phone was the Russian ambassador's chief aide for cultural affairs—which meant the top Red spy in America.

"Commrade Valashnikov, you are to leave immediately," he said without preamble.

"Leave? But why?"

"Why? Why? Is there a change in the policy that you ask me why?"

"But I've found what I came to find. It's here. It's here. After ten years I've found it," said Valashnikov.

"Yes. You may have. You may also have caused an international incident. You may endanger détente, and without détente, without friendship, without mutual understanding, how can we ever make the surprise attack? Valashnikov, you are a fool, and you are to leave immediately."

Valashnikov breathed deeply. He was just too close to success to lose gracefully. "Would you mind telling me what I am supposed to have done?"

"Gladly," said the chief aide for cultural affairs.

"First, your assault on that little girl, that little Indian child—has exposed you to criminal charges and our nation to embarrassment."

"But . . ."

"Do not 'but' me. If you were just a pervert, that would be bad enough. But you are a fool. To think that you have offered Russian arms to the Indians at Wounded Elk! You have tampered with an internal American problem. You have involved us in an affairs we should not be involved in."

"But, I never . . ."

"Do not deny it, Valashnikov. I have heard it myself, with my own ears, just moments ago. You are just lucky the mayor of Wounded Elk is a reasonable man. Mayor Van Riker will not press charges."

"Van Riker? He's a . . ."

"He is an elected official, Valashnikov. An elected official. And would an American mayor lie? You will leave immediately. You will return to Vladivostok and wait there until you hear from us."

The phone clicked sharply in Valashnikov's ear.

Imbeciles! Stupid, foolish imbeciles! They had been duped by Van Riker. Somehow he had gotten information on Valashnikov, and he had used that information to give the ring of truth to the rest of the story he had told the Russian Embassy. And the embassy had believed it.

Stupid. Well, they could be as stupid as they wished, but Valashnikov would not help them in their stupidity. For ten years he had been right and he had been punished for his beliefs and for KGB stupidity. And now that he was on the verge of success, of redemption, he would not be cheated out of it by a spy in Washington who believed a ridiculous, incredible story.

In Moscow they must learn that Valashnikov had been right. There was nothing else left in life for him. His life had been struggles and losses, but he had to balance the books this time. He had to prove he was right.

Leave now? Go back to Vladivostok and his clerk's job? No! Even if he had wished to, he knew he would never have reached Vladivostok. Anyone believed to be fool enough to tamper with American politics would be exiled—or shot.

Valashnikov put his pistol into a dresser drawer, donned his jacket, and walked out of his room. He would find a way to show Russia he was right.

When Remo came back along the road from the Apowa village, he was not stopped by the federal marshals, who all seemed to be congregated around the large tent that was being used as press headquarters.

Remo strolled over in that direction and saw that the TV lights were on, cameras were humming, and the pen-and-pencil reporters were hastily scribbling notes. The center of all the attention was a face Remo recognized immediately. It had graced the covers of news magazines. It had been magnified forty times and seen on motion picture screens around the world. It was Perkin Marlowe. The actor wore blue jeans and a T-shirt, and his thinning, longish light brown hair was caught in a small pony tail.

"Genocidal America," he said softly, his lips hardly moving.

"What'd he say?" one of the reporters yelled. "What'd he say?"

"Homicidal America," said another reporter.

"Thanks," said the first, happy he hadn't missed anything.

Perkin Marlowe went on, answering questions in a voice so dull and diffused that it was difficult to understand. But the thrust was that America was an evil country and Americans were evil, dull, stupid people who did not have the good sense to support this obviously worthwhile cause of the honest, free, nature-loving red man.

That the same evil, dull, stupid American people had made Perkin Marlowe rich by attending his films he did not deem worthy of mention, and if any of the reporters thought of it, they did not mention it either, lest they seem to their peers to be establishment stooges.

"I am on my way to the RIP encampment," Marlowe said. "There I will make my stand alongside my Indian brothers though we may fall under the onslaught of the government troops."

"What troops?" called out Remo before slipping to a different spot in the crowd.

Marlowe looked confused. "Everybody knows there are troops hidden all around here."

"That's right," squeaked Jerry Candler. "I had it in the *Globe*. Be quiet there in back."

Marlowe continued, "Yes, we may fall under the onslaught, but we will fight bravely."

"Forget the fight," Remo called. "Did you remember to bring more booze?" The last truckload's all gone."

Again he moved before anyone could spot him. Marlowe looked around, trying to find the speaker. Finally he said, "Gentlemen, I think that's all. If I never see any of you again, keep up the good work. Fight the good fight."

He turned quickly and as Candler led the audience in applause, walked rapidly from the press tent and across the grass prairie toward the church.

The newsmen followed him, lugging their equipment. The marshals moved along with the crowd, across the field toward the church.

And unseen on the main road, headed from the motel to the monument was Valashnikov.

Remo, who did not see him, went back to the motel. He found Chiun in lotus position on the floor, looking through the large front window.

Chiun quickly rose to his feet. "You have been gone so long. Did you like him? Isn't he nice?"

"How much did he offer you?"

"Well, it wasn't just me," Chiun said. "He would want you, too. And he would pay you something, also."

"How nice," said Remo. "Chiun, I'm surprised at you."

"I tried, Remo. I told him to be sure to pay you a lot; otherwise your feelings would be hurt."

"Not that, Chiun. Trusting the Russians. You know how you don't trust the Chinese? The Russians are worse."

161

"I have never heard that of them," said Chiun.

"No? Did you talk to him about television?"

Chiun raised an eyebrow. "Television? Why should I talk to him about television? I am not an anchor person. What is an anchor person, anyway?"

"An anchor person is a person who sinks a news show with heavy attempts at humor," said Remo. "What I'm talking about is your daytime dramas. What are you going to watch instead of 'As the Planet Revolves'?"

"Why instead of?" asked Chiun.

"Because Russia doesn't have 'As the Planet Revolves,'" said Remo.

"You lie," said Chiun, his face whitening as the blood drained.

"No, Little Father, it is true. Russia does not have the soaps."

"He told me they did."

"He lied."

"Are you sure? Are you not just being patriotic because you do not want to work for Mother Russia?"

"Ask him again."

"I will."

Chiun led the way out of the room. They marched to Valashnikov's room, and Chiun pounded on the door. When there was no answer, he put his right hand on the doorknob and removed it. Slowly the door swung open. Chiun peered inside.

"He is not here."

"Good thing for him," said Remo, looking at the doorknob still in Chiun's hand.

"We will find him. There are only two places to be.

162

Around here, you are either in your room or out of your room. That's all."

As they walked down the concrete ribbon in front of the rooms, General Van Riker stepped from his room, a satisfied smile on his face.

"Have you seen him?" asked Chiun.

"Seen whom?"

"The rascal Russian with the foolish name," said Chiun.

"Valashnikov," said Remo.

"No," said Van Riker. "He may be on his way back to Russia by now."

"We will see," said Chiun and turned, leading the way from the motel toward the monument.

The press was disappointed. Perkin Marlowe had simply vanished into the Episcopal church, and Dennis Petty had denied the reporters admittance.

"When we want you, we'll rattle your chain," he said.

"But we're covering the story for the whole world," protested Jonathan Bouchek.

"Shove the whole world," said Petty, slamming the church door in their faces.

The reporters just looked at each other.

"He must have terrible pressures on him," said Jerry Candler.

"Yes," agreed another reporter. "Still, he didn't have to be rude."

"Noooo," said Candler, "but he's been dealing with the government for so long, I guess it's hard to act any other way."

There were nods of agreement, and the press, having convinced itself that Petty's arrogance was somehow Washington's fault, turned and strolled away from the church toward the monument.

Valashnikov was already there. So this was it. The Cassandra. The evil machine that had cost him his career, his future, his happiness. What else could it cost him?

He looked at the bronze plaque over the center of the raised marble slab. It was ingenious, he thought. Van Riker had designed it well.

Slowly Valashnikov walked around the monument. In the bushes toward the back he spotted a shiny object. He dropped to his knees and brought out a piece of metal, the part Van Riker had removed to disarm the missile.

Valashnikov held it in his hands, looking at it carefully, his body already absorbing its deadly radiation. But he was happy that he recognized it as the bridging unit needed to fire the Cassandra.

Without it, he realized, Cassandra could not work. It could not move. If hit, it might explode, but it would explode in America, not in Russia. America was vulnerable, after all. He must get the message back to Moscow. He must let them know!

Up ahead he saw the press approaching. He waved to them. He did not see the group approaching from behind—Remo, Chiun, and Van Riker.

"There he is. There is the devil," said Chiun. "You are not lying to me, Remo?" he asked.

"No, Little Father. Would I lie?"

"Hmmmmm."

Valashnikov lifted his hulk up onto the monument. He held the missing part of the Cassandra over his head, waving it at the reporters.

"Over here!" he yelled. "Over here!"

The reporters stopped and stared at the strange fat man dancing on the monument. He kept waving to them with the missile part.

"Come quick!" he called. "Evidence of American warmongering."

"We'd better hurry," said Candler. "He may have something."

"Start shooting," said Jonathan Bouchek to his cameraman, and as the reporters moved toward Valashnikov, cameras began to whir and tape recorders to hum.

Valashnikov looked at his hands and saw the flesh reddening. No matter. He would do his job for Mother Russia. He danced up and down on the monument, waving to the press. "Hurry! Quick!" he shouted.

"What's he doing?" Remo asked.

Van Riker was looking. "Damnit," he said, "he's got the missile part. He knows Cassandra's disarmed."

"So what?" asked Remo.

"So, Russia will know, too. Any technician who sees that part in Valashnikov's hands will know that missile won't fly. The doomsday defense is done. America's vulnerable."

Chiun ignored the conversation. Resolutely he marched to the marble base of the monument. Up above his head Valashnikov was still jumping up and down and yelling.

"Hey, you!" called Chiun.

Valashnikov looked down.

"Tell me the truth. Do you have 'As the Planet Revolves' on your television?"

"No," said Valashnikov.

"You lied to me."

"It was necessary for the good of the state."

"It's not nice to fool the master of Sinanju."

Meanwhile Remo had moved around in front of the monument and was holding off the press, which had approached to within thirty feet of the marble slab.

"Sorry, fellas, you can't come any closer."

"Why not?"

"Radioactivity," Remo said.

"I knew it, I knew it!" exclaimed Candler. "The government's planning to use nuclear weapons on the Indian liberators."

"Right," said Remo. "And after that we're going to firebomb jaywalkers."

The cameras kept grinding at Valashnikov as he roared, "I am Russian spy. This is missile to blow up world. It works no longer. It broken. This part make it work no more."

He waved the part over his head like a lasso, then jumped to the ground, dropping the shiny metal onto the dirt. He looked down at his hands. The flesh was blistering, burning before his eyes, the fluid under it boiling.

He looked up at General Van Riker, who was staring sadly at him. "I have won, General," Valashnikov said triumphantly.

Van Riker did not answer.

"They will see film in Russia and know that Cassandra no longer works."

He wheeled as Chiun grabbed his shoulder.

"Why did you lie to me?" Chiun demanded.

"I had to. I am sorry, old man. But not too sorry. I have won. I have won." His face beamed with happiness. "Russia knows where Cassandra is. I have won."

"We will see," hissed Chiun.

He darted under the tarpaulin that still lay in front of the marble monument. The canvas began to rise and fall as Chiun moved under it. It looked as if children were playing under a blanket.

"We want to talk to that Russian spy," said Bouchek to Remo.

"You can't," said Remo, being careful to keep his face twisted in a grimace that made him unrecognizable. "He's an escaped lunatic. He might be dangerous."

"What is all this radioactivity crap?" asked another reporter.

"Top secret. I can't tell you," said Remo.

Behind him he heard the slap of hands, sharp clicking sounds that he realized came from Chiun's fingernails.

He glanced over his shoulder occasionally and finally saw Chiun came back out from under the tarpaulin. Chiun pulled the heavy canvas away from the black marble slab, which seemed undamaged except for a small, thin crack in a section along the top.

167

Van Riker was talking to Valashnikov. "You *have* won, you know."

"Thank you, General," said the Russian. His heart was racing now, and the fire in his hands was building to incredible agony. "How long do I live?"

"You held that activator for how long?"

"Ten minutes."

Van Riker just shook his head. "Sorry."

"I must be sure my victory is complete." Valashnikov turned toward the newsmen, but between him and them was Chiun.

"If you want a complete victory, I have one for you," said Chiun.

"Yes?"

"You want to prove to Russia that this is the Cassandra?"

"Yes."

"All right," said Chiun. "Up there you will see a crack in the marble at the top of the monument. Go push on it."

The cameras whirred as Valashnikov, staggering from the poison of radioactivity flooding his body and his brain, moved forward to the marble monument. His mind seemed to bubble with thoughts of its own. He fought to keep control of the ideas and images that whirled behind his eyes.

"I Russian spy," he bawled. "This American capitalist missile."

He reached the spot Chiun had pointed out. He stumbled, and fell against it. A section of the marble block moved away, revealing a new section of the marble beneath it.

Valashnikov saw it as he fell. "No, no," he whimpered. "No, no." And then he was still. The cameras whirred and newsmen crowded around his lifeless body, which lay in front of a marble legend that read:

CASSANDRA 2.

CHAPTER FIFTEEN

The reporters looked at each other.

"What's Cassandra 2?" Jonathan Bouchek asked Remo.

"A secret missile designed to blow up the entire world," Candler answered for him.

Bouchek turned to him. "Do you know that for a fact?"

"What else could it be?" said Candler. "What else . . ."

He stopped as they heard the first noise. It sounded like a faint wind blowing from the east, and then it increased in intensity and pitch, as if it were growing stronger, coming nearer. It was behind them and they turned.

And then they saw the source of the noise.

At the crest of the mesa upon which the Apowa village of Wounded Elk was located, one man became visible. Then another. Then another. Then clusters of them. And soon the entire edge of the bluff was filled with men on horseback, shoulder to shoulder. They wore feathers and war paint. They were naked to the waist, and across their backs they had strapped guns and bows. Now they stopped to look down the half-mile toward the church, where the RIP members were drinking peacefully, and then one man in the center, astride a pinto pony, waved his rifle over his head, and with an earth-shattering scream, the Apowa braves came charging down the hillside on their ponies, heading for the church.

Remo smiled to himself. Brandt was not going to be cheated out of his revenge by any old bent cannon.

"It's the Indians attacking," one reporter cried.

"Don't be fooled. It's probably green berets in disguise," said Candler. "Why would Indians attack the RIP forces who are seeking justice for all red men?"

"That's true," said Jonathan Bouchek. "Let's go," he told his cameraman, and they began trotting along the road from the monument to the church. Other reporters broke into a run and followed.

The Apowa warriors, two hundred strong, were now down off the hill and galloping across the open prairie toward the church, their banshee wails filling the prairie.

The noise brought the church to life, too. Inside, the RIP members were celebrating the arrival of Perkin Marlowe with a cocktail party at which the most popular drink was Scotch with Scotch on the side. Dennis Petty heard the sound first.

"Getting so noisy around here, you can't even have a good party," he said, tossing an empty bottle at the corner of the altar, where it fell and cracked again a pile of bottles. Then, drink in hand, he strolled to the front of the church. "Perkin, old Kemosabe, make

171

yourself a drink." he said. He opened the front door of the church and looked out. "Holy shit," he whistled.

"What is it?" called Lynn Cosgrove, who sat in a nearby pew taking notes.

"It's Indians," said Petty. "Hey, it's Indians," he yelled to the entire church. "*Real* Indians."

"Probably planning to rape all us women," said Cosgrove.

"Hey! Shit! They're coming here," Petty yelled. "They're coming here."

"What are they yelling" asked Marlowe, moving toward Petty.

"They're yelling, 'Kill RIP. Kill RIP.' Shit. Sheeeit! I'm getting out of here."

"They're government lackies," said Cosgrove without turning.

"Right," said Perkin Marlowe.

"Government lackies, my ass. They're Indians. Real Indians. I ain't screwing around with no real Indians," Petty said.

By now all forty RIP members had moved to Petty's side.

"Shit is right," said one of them. "They look mean. I'm getting out of here."

"Let's go," said Petty. "Before one of us gets hurt."

They started down the steps of the church and broke into a run toward the line of federal marshals.

As they ran, Petty ripped off his dirty T-shirt and waved it over his head. "Sanctuary!" he screamed. "We surrender. Sanctuary."

The other RIP members followed his lead, ripping off their shirts, waving them over their heads.

"Help! Protect us! Sanctuary!" Beer bottles and whiskey flasks dropped from their pockets as they ran.

The reporters made the mistake of trying to head them off and were trampled.

"Get out of my way, you nitwit bastards," shouted Petty, slamming a straight arm into Jerry Candler and stepping on Jonathan Bouchek.

Finally convinced and bringing up the rear of the RIP stampede, but gaining ground every minute, was Perkin Marlowe. He was whimpering, "I just wanted to help. I just wanted to help. Don't let me get hurt."

In an instant the RIP members were past the press. Candler lifted himself up on one elbow and looked at the fleeing figures. He turned to Bouchek, who lay on his back in the dust. "Can't blame him for panicking. I mean, after all, he's under terrible pressures, with those disguised soldiers after him, trying to kill him."

Candler looked up and saw a man on a pinto pony standing over him. The man was red-skinned and wore a headdress of feathers. He held a rifle loosely in his right hand.

"Who are you?" the man asked.

Candler scrambled to his feet. "I'm glad you asked. I'm Jerry Candler of the *New York Globe* and I know what you think your game is, but you're not going to get away with it, terrifying those poor Indians like that."

"You mean all those Indians from Chicago's South Side?" asked Brandt, looking down from his pony.

"The world will hear about this atrocity," said Candler.

"Were you born a fool, or did you study it in school?" asked Brandt. He looked up and saw the RIP members had crossed the line of federal marshals and were surrendering as fast as the marshals could get to them. Then he turned to the rest of his war party. "Come, men. Let's go and clean the garbage out of our church."

They turned their ponies and trotted away. Candler began walking toward the marshals, already composing the lead for his Sunday column: "Vietnam. Attica. San Francisco. And now Wounded Elk joints the long list of American atrocities."

Remo had watched the charge and the near battle from a seat atop the marble monument. He felt satisfied at its outcome and turned to get Chiun's reaction. But Chiun was deep in discussion with Van Riker. "There," Chiun was saying. "There is the weapon you would have invented, had you any brains."

"What do you mean?" asked Van Riker. "You've just let the world know that this is Cassandra."

Chiun shook his head. "This is Cassandra 2. It says so on the plaque I made. That means there is a Cassandra 1, and no enemy will be able to find it, and it will not hurt anyone, either."

Van Riker looked confused. "The Russians?"

"The Russians will be more sure that Cassandra 1

exists because they have seen parts from Cassandra 2. I have made for you the perfect weapon. Harmless but effective. The only kind white men should be allowed to play with."

Van Riker's tanned face opened into a slow smile. "You know, you're right." He looked toward the marble slab, where the dead Valashnikov lay, and shook his head. "I feel sorry for him in a way. All those years he spent finding this missile, and then, when he does, he loses anyway."

"Pfffffui," said Chiun. "Death is too good for him. There is no man lower than a man who lies to an assassin about his wages."

Together, the three men walked back to the motel, where Van Riker immediately got busy. He called Washington, and ordered nuclear crews in to dismantle Cassandra 2. He did it on an open line and talked to every clerk who answered the telephone, just to make sure his orders were not only intercepted but given the widest possible public distribution.

Van Riker smiled. He could talk about Cassandra 2 all he wanted now. He had the perfect weapon— Cassandra 1.

Remo sat in the next room with Chiun. It was still too early for the day's soap operas, so they watched the news. It was filled with shots of Valashnikov and Cassandra 2 and the Apowa attack on the church and the RIP members being routed.

Jonathan Bouchek shoved a camera and a microphone in the face of Lynn Cosgrove. "Burning Star . . ." he began.

"My name is Cosgrove," she said. "Lynn Cosgrove."

"But I thought your Indian name was . . ."

"That was a past chapter in my history. The Indian struggles have come and gone. Today there is a new and greater struggle confronting all Americans. The struggle for sexual liberation. I have here the outline of my new book." She waved a notebook at him. "It will point the way to honest healthy sexual relationships among all people. Prudery must die." She reached her free hand up to the neck of her buckskin dress and ripped it open, baring her breasts for cameras. "What's wrong with screwing?" she yelled. "Sex, now and forever."

Behind her, a voice yelled, "Sakajawea. Sakajawea."

It was Dennis Petty.

Lynn Cosgrove wheeled and yelled back, "Fraud bastard. Fake, phoney, chicken shit fraud bastard." As Bouchek's crew kept filming, Petty grabbed his crotch with his right hand and thrust it forward toward Cosgrove. "That for you."

Watching his live air presentation degenerate into an X-rated display of obscene gestures, Bouchek sank slowly to the ground. Before cutting away, the last shot the camera got was of Bouchek crying, his makeup washing down his cheeks.

The program switched back to the studio for an announcement by the minority-party senator that he would introduce a bill in the Senate to pay twenty-five thousand dollars to each of the surviving members of what he called "the new Wounded Elk massacre."

Remo slapped off the television set. "Well, Little Father, the nation lives."

"I can tell," said Chiun. "Insanity still runs amuck."

"Speaking of insanity, I'd better call Smith."

Smith listened quietly to Remo's explanation of the day's events, and since he did not criticize Remo's actions, Remo took that to mean everything had worked out well.

"You have one more thing to do, you remember," said Smith.

"I know," said Remo.

He hung up and walked through the connecting doors into Van Riker's room.

Van Riker was just hanging up his phone. He turned, and when he saw Remo, he smiled, rubbing his hands together.

"Well, everything's in good order," he said. "The Pentagon's going to leak a story about a string of Cassandras hidden around the world. Crews will be here to dismantle this one. All in all, I'd say a pretty good day." He looked at Remo and smiled. "So what do you say we get on with it?"

"On with what?" asked Remo.

"You've come to kill me. I know to much . . . about you, the Oriental, Smith, and CURE."

"Why didn't you run?" asked Remo.

"Remember those two bodies in the monuments? I had to do that to keep Cassandra a secret. You have to do the same thing. Why run? You'd get me."

"That's right. I would," said Remo.

"Give Smith my best wishes. He's a brilliant man," said Van Riker.

"I will," said Remo and quickly killed the tanned general. He arranged the body on the bed so it would look like Van Riker had died from a heart attack caused by excitement, then went back into his own room.

"Well, Little Father, we should be leaving."

Chiun was at the dresser, writing with a straight pen on a long piece of parchment.

"As soon as I am done with this."

"What is it you're doing?"

"It is a letter to the Mad Emperor Smith. I think I should be paid for the creation of Cassandras 1 and 2. Creating weapons is outside the contract and should be paid for." He turned to Remo. "Especially since I turned down a very attractive offer from Mother Russia."

SPIES, INTRIGUE, ADVENTURE—

THE BEST READING FROM PINNACLE BOOKS!

BOMB RUN, by Spencer Dunmore. An excitingly written story about a bomb run over Berlin in 1944, the thirtieth and final mission for one British Bomber Command air crew. They will take off tonight, make a last passage through the barrage of flak and flame, take a last gamble against the Messerschmitts, and return to England and relative peace. But across the Channel, a young German fighter pilot, grieving for his dead parents and thinking of the combat to come, is destined to alter forever the lives of the bomber pilot and his crew. A thrilling and compelling novel.   **P116   95¢**

SABERLEGS, by Eric Pace. An incredible tale of intrigue, woven by one of the *New York Times'* top foreign correspondents, as scaringly possible as it is exciting. The mission of Charles Randall: to get Von Zugen, the sadistic German scientist who invented a lethal weapon for Hitler, escaped with it at the war's end, and now wants to sell it to Arab commandos for use against Israel. A story taut with suspense and tender with half-realized love—a brilliantly constructed spy novel.

P061   95¢

OVER THE WALL, by Duncan Thorp. A suspenseful adventure of revolution and assassination. There are only six people in the group—one a woman—who plan to ignite the take-over of a Caribbean island. They are up against a brutal and powerful dictator whose rule has been absolute and impregnable. The fight for leadership among the six is almost as exciting and intriguing as the revolution they foment. Romance, sex and action for the most demanding adventure aficionado!   **P101   95¢**

THE ELECTION, by Sherwin Markman. What happens when an exciting presidential election is tied, and the final decision is thrown into the House of Representatives. Heightening the complications and tensions, too, are the simultaneous riots of black militants across the country. America is in chaos! The pivotal figure in this melee is Stu Brady, a young assistant press secretary. Stu becomes the liaison man between the major candidates, as scandal and intrigue come to the boiling point. An election you'll never forget! **P100 $1.50**

CLASH OF DISTANT THUNDER, by A. C. Marin. A spy story you'll find difficult to put down; impossible to forget. The spy, Dr. John Wells. His assignment, to find a missing informant in Paris. This misplaced agent may have defected or may have been a double agent right along. Or he may have been loyal— but has been caught and silenced. Wells is the hunted as well as the hunter, from Paris to Switzerland and Italy. A wild chase of shadows and suspense. **P064 95¢**

THE MOST POPULAR AND BESTSELLING NON-FICTION FROM PINNACLE BOOKS

BURN AFTER READING, by Ladislas Farago. Here are the spy-masters, the heroes, the traitors, and all the cryptic subtlety and horrific violence that marked their grim activities. The more gripping because it really happened—it's all fascinating, particularly if you bear in mind that the same sort of thing is going on right this minute, as clandestinely and just as ruthlessly. By the author of GAME OF THE FOXES and PATTON. Fast-moving, smoothly written, yet fully documented.   **PO90   95¢**

THE CANARIS CONSPIRACY, by Roger Manvell and Heinrich Fraenkel. An astounding chronicle of the plot to kill Hitler. This is the documented story of the work of Admiral Wilhelm Canaris' Department Z, pieced together from the accounts of survivors and told in full for the first time. This group attempted to liquidate Hitler in order to make peace with the allies, but before the plotters could achieve their goal, the conspiracy was discovered and broken by arrests, executions and suicides. One of the most incredible stories to come out of World War II.
PO93 $1.25

DIVINE THUNDER, by Bernard Millot. This is the story of the kamikazes, the suicide pilots of Japan during World War II, and of why, when the need arose, they were ready to die without hesitation. In both soldiers and civilians, a mystical reverence for the homeland was almost second nature. The author describes their devastating assaults and the American reaction to them and he reveals what made the kamikazes men of such strange grandeur and heroism. With original drawings.
P108 $1.25

THE KENNEDY WOMEN, by Pearl S. Buck. Here are the fascinating and extraordinary women of the Kennedy family. With the skill of a journalist, the artistry of a gifted storyteller, and the seasoned eye of a biographer, Pearl S. Buck paints a portrait in words of the women who bear the most famous family names in history. From Rose, the durable and dynamic matriarch, to JFK's young Caroline—and including Kathleen, Rosemary, Patricia, Jean, Eunice, Ethel, Joan and Jacqueline—these are the ladies of our times.   **P113 $1.50**

BUGSY, by George Carpozi, Jr. The wild but true story of Benjamin "Bugsy" Siegel. By the time he was twenty-one, this handsome hoodlum had done almost everything a professional mobster could do. It was Bugsy Siegel who transformed a sandy wasteland into Las Vegas. The same Bugsy Siegel who hobnobbed with Hollywood's royalty and was treated almost as a king himself. He traveled widely, ate in the finest restaurants, and owned an estate in Beverly Hills. His women were legion. But never far beneath the surface was a hard-eyed killer—a killer who died as violently as he lived.   **P244 $1.25**

MICKEY COHEN: MOBSTER, by Ed Reid. Finally—the brutal truth about a well-known gangster! This is a story that Mickey Cohen would rather *not* have told, but a story that can no longer be kept secret. Mickey Cohen is a man who has always been larger than life, who is part of the social history of our time. He's a member of the Jewish Mafia, who has lived hard and lived flamboyantly; who brags about deeds most would want hidden; whose friends have been jet-setters, criminals, evangelists, film stars, politicians, and members of the Hollywood social scene. Right now, he's down but not out, and don't ever count him *out!* Not until the end.   **P257 $1.25**

SUSAN HAYWARD: THE DIVINE BITCH, by Doug McClelland. The triumphs and tragedies of a fiery and talented screen star. Susan Hayward has lived a life to pale even her most vivid screen roles. There were two marriages, twin sons, and constant strife that persists to this day. She was a feminist before the fashion—with femininity plus and a drive to achieve that led her far from the Brooklyn tenement where she began her life. This is the first book ever on one of the First Ladies of the movies' Golden Age: Susan Hayward.   **P276 $1.25**

INSIDE ADOLF HITLER, by Roger Manvell and Heinrich Fraenkel. This is *not* a book about politics. It is *not* a book about warfare. What is it then? It is a book about the mind of a man, a probing portrait into the personality development of the most hated man of the 20th century. **INSIDE ADOLF HITLER** is by two of the most renowned Third Reich historians. Their most recent books, *The Canaris Conspiracy* and *The Men Who Tried To Kill Hitler,* have sold millions. Here, for the first time, is an in-depth analysis of the public and private personalities of Adolf Hitler.   **P277 $1.50**

STAND BY TO DIE, by A. V. Sellwood. The heroic story of a lone, embattled WW II ship. It was a small Yangtse river steamer, manned by a makeshift crew of fugitives. She sailed from war-torn Singapore to do battle with the armed might of a Japanese fleet. It was an epic naval action. Heroism was the order of the day. There were no lean British cruisers to divert the Japanese guns, there were no RAF planes to provide air cover. Just one bullet-riddled tub that wouldn't say die! The story could have been lost forever, as it has been for many years, had not A. V. Sellwood pieced together the almost unbelievable story of "the most decorated small ship in the navy."　　　　　　　　　　　　　　　　**P171　95¢**

SIEGE AND SURVIVAL: THE ODYSSEY OF A LENINGRADER, by Elena Skrjabina. A diary of one of the most devastating sieges in history. During the siege of Leningrad which began on September 8, 1941, nearly one-and-one-half million people died—of hunger, of cold, of disease, from German bullets and bombs. Elena Skrjabina survived. She endured. This book is a record of that experience, and it has been acclaimed by critics everywhere. *Publishers Weekly* said that it is "written in unadorned but eloquent prose that is remarkably effecting." *Bestsellers* said "It is human."　　　　　　　　　**P199　95¢**

VIZZINI!, by Sal Vizzini, with Oscar Fraley and Marshall Smith. The secret lives of our most successful narc! Sal Vizzini may die because he wrote this book. He was formerly an undercover agent for the Federal Bureau of Narcotics—an assignment which took him to Naples, where he became a "friend" of exiled Mafia chieftain Charles "Lucky" Luciano; to Burma, where he blew up a heroin factory; to Lebanon, where he outwitted a Communist gun-running ring; and to Atlanta, Georgia, where he posed as a con in the Federal pen. He was shot three times, knifed twice, beaten nearly to death, and had several contracts put out by the Mafia to kill him. Many of the men now in jail will learn for the first time who put them there.　　　　　　　　　　　　　　　　　　　**P226　$1.25**

WALKING TALL, by Doug Warren. The true story of Buford Pusser, a sheriff who has become a living legend. Buford is an honest man, a good man, he has tried to clean out the criminal element of his community. In doing so he has been shot eight times, stabbed five, rammed by a speeding car, had his home fire bombed, and was trapped in an ambush that killed his wife. But, Buford still lives. He raided the prostitution houses, the gambling dens and illicit moonshine stills and almost single handedly ousted crooked officials. His story has been made into a major motion picture by Cinerama.　　　　**P478　$1.25**

This is your Order Form . . .
Just clip and mail.

_____ P090	BURN AFTER READING, Ladislas Farago	.95
_____ P093	THE CANARIS CONSPIRACY, Manvell & Fraenkel	1.25
_____ P108	DIVINE THUNDER, Bernard Millot	1.25
_____ P113	THE KENNEDY WOMEN, Pearl S. Buck	1.50
_____ P171	STAND BY TO DIE, A. V. Sellwood	.95
_____ P199	SIEGE & SURVIVAL, Elena Skrjabina	.95
_____ P226	VIZZINI, Sal Vizzini, with Fraley & Smith	1.25
_____ P478	WALKING TALL, Doug Warren	1.25
_____ P244	BUGSY, George Carpozi, Jr.	1.25
_____ P257	MICKEY COHEN: MOBSTER, Ed Reid	1.25
_____ P276	SUSAN HAYWARD: THE DIVINE BITCH, Doug McClelland	1.25
_____ P277	INSIDE ADOLF HITLER, Manvell & Fraenkel	1.50

TO ORDER

Please check the space next to book/s you want, send this order form together with your check or money order, include the price of the book/s and 25¢ for handling and mailing, to:

PINNACLE BOOKS, INC. / P.O. Box 4347,
Grand Central Station / New York, N.Y. 10017

☐ CHECK HERE IF YOU WANT A FREE CATALOG.

I have enclosed $_____check_____or money order_____
as payment in full. No C.O.D.'s.

Name_____

Address_____

City_____State_____Zip_____
(Please allow time for delivery.)